USBORNE

Sandy Lane Stables

*More great Sandy Lane stories
for you to read:*

The Midnight Horse

Michelle Bates

USBORNE

First published in 1997 by Usborne Publishing Ltd, Usborne House,
83-85 Saffron Hill, London EC1N 8RT, England.
www.usborne.com

This is a work of fiction. The character, incidents, and dialogues are
products of the author's imagination and are not to be construed as real.
Any resemblance to actual events or persons, living or dead,
is entirely coincidental.

First published in America 1998. AE

ISBN 0 7945 0506 6 (paperback)

Typeset in Times

Printed in Great Britain

Editor: Susannah Leigh
Series Editor: Gaby Waters
Designer: Lucy Parris
Cover Design: Neil Francis
Map Illustrations by: John Woodcock
Cover Photograph supplied by: Horsepix

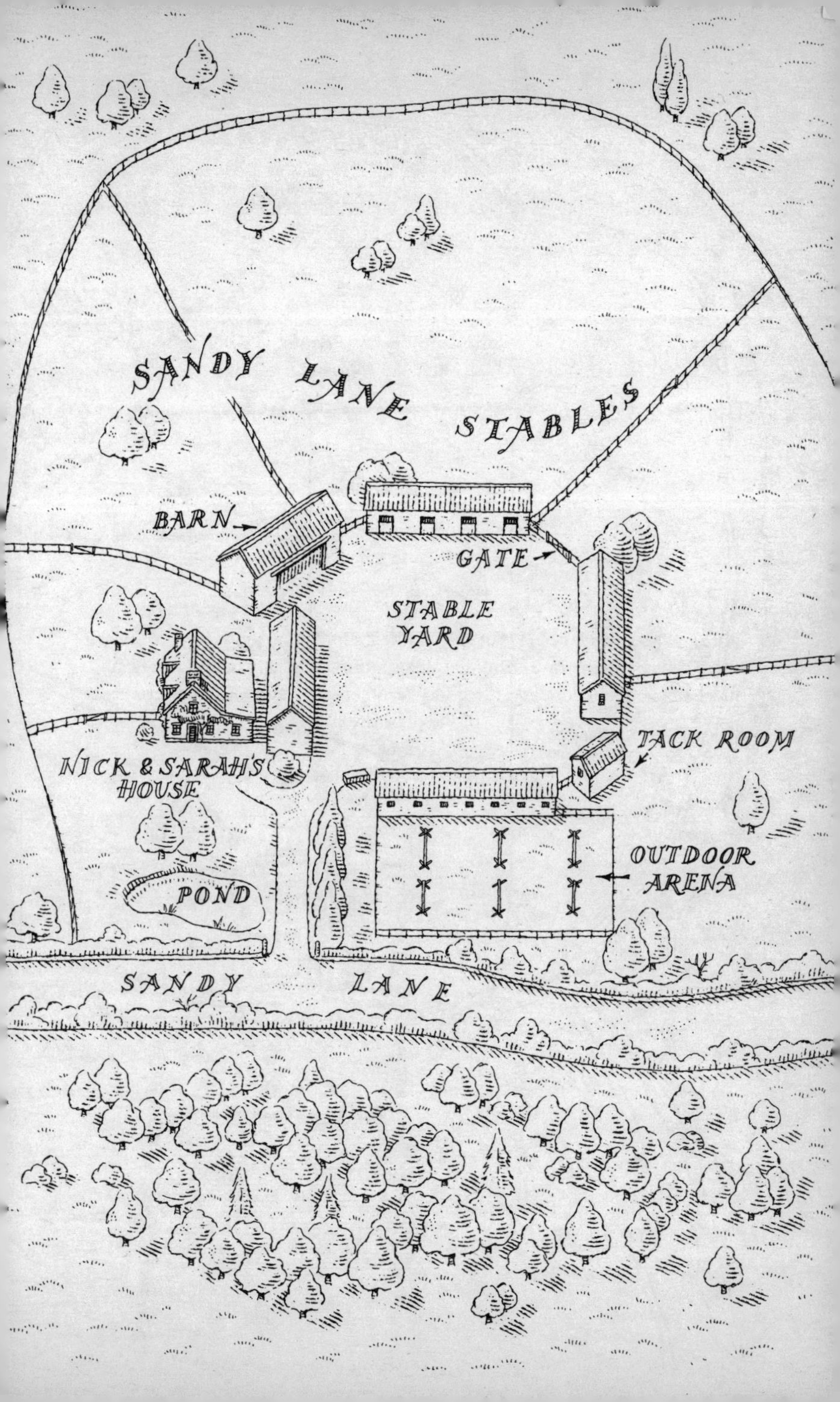

SANDY LANE STABLES

BARN

GATE

STABLE YARD

NICK & SARAH'S HOUSE

TACK ROOM

POND

OUTDOOR ARENA

SANDY LANE

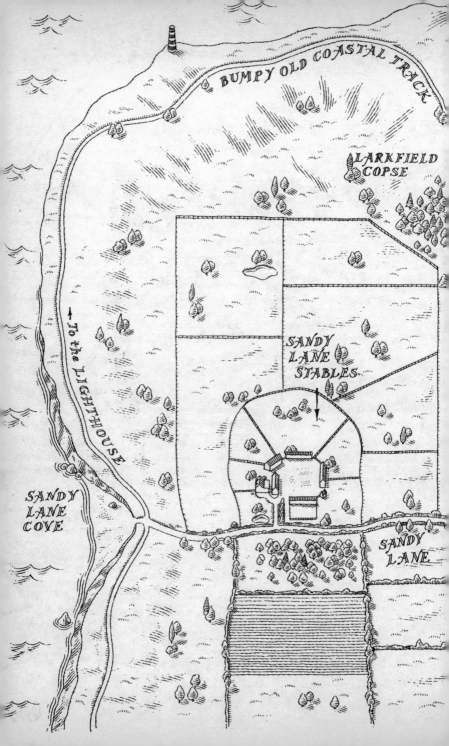

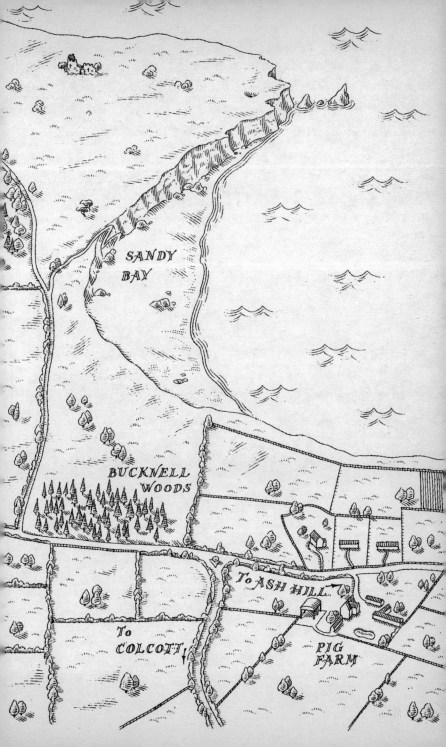

SANDY BAY

BUCKNELL WOODS

To ASH HILL

To COLCOTT

PIG FARM

CONTENTS

1

IZZY

The horse cantered gracefully around the paddock in long, easy strides, his tail held high, the crest of his neck arched. His jet-black coat contrasted sharply with the white frost; his hooves hardly seemed to touch the ground as he danced forward. On his back sat a girl, light and balanced, coaxing the reins through her fingers. Effortlessly they perfected a figure eight. The horse's ears were pricked as they drew to a halt. It was dusk, and the light was fading. Shivering, the rider swung herself out of the saddle and jumped to the ground.

"That's enough for tonight, Midnight," she said rubbing her hands together for warmth. "Or we won't be able to see a thing." Gently, she pushed the horse's nose away as his head cradled forward for a treat.

"I don't have anything for you right now," she

smiled, leading him off through the fields by the reins. The horse snorted, as if in response, his breath spiraling into the winter air like smoke.

Anyone who happened to pass by would have thought there was little out of the ordinary about the pair. The girl could have been any one of a number of riders exercising her horse in the evening hours after school. Colcott and the surrounding countryside were horsy territory. But things were a little different for Izzy Paterson and Midnight. He wasn't hers to begin with and in just over a week's time he was due to be sold...

"A new start for us all." That was what Izzy's father had said the summer before last, when he'd given up his job as a journalist to move to the country and write his first book. And when the idea had first been announced, Izzy had hardly been able to contain herself. A move to the country spelled out one thing to her – more horses.

Izzy had been horse-crazy for as long as she could remember. But living in the city meant that Izzy had to content herself with the weekly riding lesson. Being in the country would change all that. Or so she thought. They'd been in Colcott about six months when Izzy had realized it wasn't going to be as simple as all that. The horse her parents had fleetingly promised her hadn't materialized and yet again Izzy found herself spending her Saturdays at just another riding stables – and not a very friendly one at that. The Elm Park Riding Stables was full of snooty girls as far as Izzy was concerned.

"When we see an improvement in your grades at school, then maybe you can have a horse, Izzy," her father had said.

But try as she might, Izzy didn't seem to be able to improve her schoolwork, and she didn't know how much longer she would be able to go on pretending to her old friends that her dream horse was on its way. Even her best friend from when she lived in the city, Alice, had given up asking about him in her letters.

And then one day back in January, all of Izzy's problems seemed to be solved. Izzy could remember the day so clearly... as if it was ingrained on her memory. The school bus had dropped her at the usual spot outside the post office and she'd happened to glance in the window. The neat writing on the postcard had jumped out at her:

Would you like to exercise a horse for free?
Rider needed in Colcott
Phone Mrs. Charlwood on 465-6783

Izzy had hardly been able to believe her eyes. Surely no one... *no one* would simply let someone ride their horse *for free*. Izzy had gone home and phoned the number immediately, sure there had to be some sort of mistake. But the offer had turned out to be genuine enough.

"My daughter, Jane, has gotten married," Mrs. Charlwood had explained. "Moved out west... Midnight's a beautiful horse. I couldn't bear to sell him. Come and try him out if you want to. I live on

3

the right-hand side of the green as you come into Colcott – the pink house with ivy."

Izzy hadn't needed a second invitation. Without hesitating, she had turned up for a tryout and almost immediately been offered the job of looking after the beautiful, part-thoroughbred horse. Well-proportioned, with graceful, sloping shoulders, Midnight was altogether in a different league from the riding school ponies Izzy was used to.

"We'll see how it goes," her mother had said when Izzy had first told her the exciting news. "I suppose at least you can give him back when you get bored with him."

Bored! As if. For nearly six months, Izzy's life had seemed complete – weekends of riding, a summer filled with horse shows. Until one day in June, Mrs. Charlwood had dropped the bombshell and announced she was emigrating to Australia at Christmas time.

Izzy had been devastated. Her whole world was collapsing before her eyes. Mrs. Charlwood had tried to make things all right – she'd even offered to give Midnight to Izzy, but Izzy's parents simply wouldn't hear of it.

"Who do you think would end up looking after him?" her mother had said. "Your father and I just can't take on that sort of responsibility at the moment. Maybe next year we'll get you your own horse, but right now it's completely out of the question."

But next year seemed a lifetime away for Izzy. A lifetime without Midnight. And now that she knew him, she didn't want just any other horse. Her parents

4

didn't understand. In fact, Mrs. Charlwood was the only one who really understood how she felt. The picture faded and Izzy found herself standing in the middle of Mrs. Charlwood's stable.

"Oh Midnight," she sighed, turning now to face the horse. "Whatever am I going to do without you?" She took a deep breath. She really had to pull herself together. It wasn't the end of the world.

But it *was* the end of the world... her world. Christmas was only a week away now, and by then Mrs. Charlwood would have gone, her house would have new owners, and Midnight would have been sold. Nothing would ever be the same again.

"Come on, we ought to put you away for the night," Izzy sighed, the light fading around her into night. "I mustn't spoil our last few days together."

Midnight tossed his head impatiently as Izzy led him off to the stables. Rounding the corner of the rambling pink house, she saw Mrs. Charlwood waving from the kitchen window. Izzy smiled weakly as they clattered across the cobblestones. Leading Midnight into his stall, she started to groom him, brushing his dark coat in swift circular movements.

"That's you all done," she said, rubbing the horse's velvety nose as she turned to put away the grooming things.

Midnight's head nodded contentedly as Izzy gave him his evening hay. With one last pat, she closed the stall door behind her and bolted the black horse in for the night. Izzy's face was strangely luminous as she turned to leave, the twilight casting an unnatural hue around her. Midnight didn't take his eyes off her. He lifted his head high over the stall door and nickered softly. Izzy felt a lump rising in her throat, almost choking her, as she tried to tear her gaze away from him. She didn't think she'd ever seen a horse quite so beautiful.

"You'll be all right Midnight. You'll soon have a new home to go to. You'll forget about me," she said, her eyes brimming with tears as she turned her bike out of Mrs. Charlwood's yard. "But I'll never forget about you," she said quietly to herself.

2

KATE

"Come on Kate! It's ten to eight! Get out of bed. You said you wanted to be at the stables early."

Kate Hardy groaned at the sound of her mother's wake-up call and hauled herself out of bed. It was the first day of Christmas break and she had things to do.

Yawning, she drew back the curtains and wandered across the room. Pulling a comb through her knotty blonde hair, Kate looked critically at the pale face that stared back at her from the mirror. Dark shadows ringed her slate-gray eyes. She was tired – a consequence of the late nights she'd spent staying up to finish her final history assignment. Still, at least she'd gotten it done. And now she didn't intend to think about it any more. For the next two weeks, the only thing she wanted to think about was her riding.

Kate and her brother, Alex, had been helping out at

Sandy Lane Stables for nearly three years now. Three years of riding, grooming, mucking out and whatever else came along. It was hard work, but they didn't mind that too much, not when it brought them nearer to horses. Besides, Nick and Sarah Brooks, the owners of the stables, really appreciated all the extra work their regular riders put in.

And this year Kate's hard work had really paid off, for she alone had been chosen to ride Sandy Lane's star horse, Feather, in the junior section at the Hawthorn Horse Trials – now just three weeks away. Made up of dressage, show jumping and cross-country, the trials were the winter event of the area and the chance Kate had been waiting for. Everyone else at the stables had excelled at some point in the past... now it was her turn. This was the chance to prove herself. Kate gritted her teeth. She was determined to do well. She really wanted to win.

Kate smiled as she thought back to Nick's parting words last night. *I think you have a real chance,* he had said. She wasn't a conceited girl. She knew that any one of the regular Sandy Lane riders would be competing had they been young enough to enter. Tom, Jess, Charlie, Rosie, even her brother Alex – all of them were better riders than she was. But they were all too old and so, Sandy Lane's hopes were riding on her.

Kate looked out of the window of the old mill her parents had converted into their home. The morning light cast a warm glow over the white garden. It had snowed heavily last night and little icicles hung precariously from the ivy-covered walls. Kate felt pleased as she gazed outside. With snow on the ground, they'd be in the all-weather outdoor ring, which spelled out one thing for Kate – more time to be spent on dressage, the discipline she liked best of all.

Quickly she glanced at her bedside clock. Five to eight. She'd been daydreaming again. She'd better get a move on. She'd said she'd be at the stables at eight to help Nick feed the horses – she was going to be late. Struggling into her britches, she grabbed her riding hat and hurried down the stairs. Alex was already up, hunched over a bowl of cereal in the kitchen.

"Mom, would you be able to give us a ride to Sandy Lane?" Kate called, pushing some bread into the toaster. "Ple-e-ase? Just this once. *It is* snowing and I'm going to be late otherwise."

Mrs. Hardy groaned. "Didn't I say a few months ago that I wouldn't run a taxi service for you and Alex? What's wrong with the bus?"

"Oh, but it'll take forever, Mom. Please," Kate begged.

Mrs. Hardy looked long and hard. "Well, just this once then, Kate. But this is the last, absolutely the *last* time," she said quickly. "You'll have to be up earlier if you want to be at the stables on time. You can't rely on me for everything."

"Thanks Mom," Kate said, scrambling around in the cupboard for the jam.

"Do you have all your Christmas presents taken care of?" Mrs. Hardy asked.

"Yes," Kate answered through a mouthful of toast,

9

mentally crossing off a check-list of the presents she had put under the tree. She smiled as she thought of the riding crop she'd bought Alex. It was beautiful – tanned leather with a shiny handle and had cost her three weeks' allowance. When she thought about how they argued, she wasn't sure he deserved it.

"Are you coming Alex?" she asked, grabbing the remains of her breakfast.

"In a minute," Alex answered.

"Well hurry up," she said urgently. "In case you didn't hear, Mom said she'll give us a lift. And I want to be there as soon as possible. *You* might not have things to do but–"

"OK, OK. Keep your hair on," Alex interrupted. "I'm just coming. I need to phone Tom first though."

"But you'll see him at the stables!" Kate cried. "Come on. We're wasting precious time."

"Oh all right." Alex reached for his jacket and headed for the door. "Let's go."

Alex and Kate hurried out of the house and crunched across the snow to the car, impatiently waiting for their mother to put the burglar alarm on.

"Here, Kate!"

Before Kate could stop him, Alex had bent down and scooped up a handful of snow.

"Come on you two. I thought you were in a hurry. Get in the car and stop messing around," Mrs. Hardy called over.

Alex and Kate brushed the snow off themselves and jumped into the car. In no time at all, Mrs. Hardy had driven them the five miles from Wakeham to the stables and dropped Kate and Alex off on Sandy Lane. As they hurried up the driveway, Kate noticed that the pond on the corner was frozen solid. She shivered and drew her collar up as she looked at her watch. Twenty five minutes after eight. They were late. Passing the line of conifers that enclosed the outdoor ring, they walked on into the stables.

Kate could see Charlie filling water buckets by the trough in the corner and Rosie and Jess were deep in conversation by the tack room. She hoped her late arrival hadn't been noticed as she hurried to get some grooming things. But it hadn't escaped Charlie and he called over to Kate as she dove into the tack room.

"Overslept did you?" he called. "Nick's been looking everywhere for you."

Kate pretended she hadn't heard him. She liked Charlie, but she wasn't in the mood for any of his sarcasm this morning. Hurrying over to Feather's stall, she drew back the bolt. The Arab mare nickered softly as Kate set to work on grooming her coat.

When she'd finished, Kate stood back to admire her handiwork. She was a perfectionist, but even she couldn't fault Feather's appearance. It was just at that moment that Nick Brooks happened to pass by.

"What happened to you this morning, Kate?" he asked.

"Sorry Nick, I overslept," Kate answered.

"Well don't worry," Nick said. "At least you've done a pretty good job on Feather. You must have used some elbow grease to get her gleaming like that. I don't think we'll risk going out over the cross-country course

1 1

in this weather," he went on. "So I'll look at your dressage test in the outdoor ring instead."

"Great," Kate answered quickly. It was as she'd hoped.

"So I'll meet you down there in five minutes, OK?" Nick went on.

"OK." Kate tacked Feather up and led the horse out of her stall. Springing neatly into the saddle, she headed off down the driveway. Feather's ears were pricked, alert and attentive, as she sniffed the air.

"All ready?" Nick grinned broadly, stamping his feet to ward off the cold as he opened the gate to let her into the ring. "Can you remember it all?" he called.

"I think so," Kate said, casting her mind back over her dressage test. In truth, she knew it like the back of her hand. She even dreamed about it in her sleep.

"Right, trot Feather around the ring to warm up and then we'll begin," Nick said. "We've got a lot of work to put in before Hawthorn," he said.

"You don't need to remind me," Kate laughed, nudging Feather on into a trot.

"Shall I start now?" she called. Nick nodded.

Tentatively, she gave the obligatory salute to the imaginary judges, feeling embarrassed that no one was there. Then she urged Feather on to make her way down the long side of the white railing at a trot. Feather didn't even falter as Kate nudged her forward and they swept across the diagonal, slicing through the center of the ring.

Kate sat deep into the saddle, feeling at ease as she brought Feather to a walk. One, two, three. Kate counted the numbers in her head before pushing Feather on into a canter. So far so good. Now just once around the ring on a free rein.

"Circle, change the rein, same on the other leg," she muttered to herself as she squeezed Feather on into a trot. Careful not to hurry the last section, she came down the center line and halted in the middle of the ring before reining back. One, two, three steps... stop. They had made it through the test easily. Riding Feather was like dancing with the perfect partner, and no matter what Nick thought, Kate had enjoyed herself. She looked up expectantly.

Nick clapped loudly. "Excellent," he said. "But what have you forgotten?"

"Er, I'm not sure," she said.

"What about the salute for the judges at the end?" he asked.

"Of course," Kate answered. "It's just so hard to remember to do it when they're not actually there."

"Well, if you get into the habit now, it'll be one less thing for you to think about that day," Nick said. "And don't look so worried," he called. "That was good. If we can get your show jumping and cross-country up to that standard, you'll be fine. I'll leave you to do a little more work on your walk to canter transitions. I have to hurry back and sign everyone in for the 10 o'clock ride."

"Yes, sure Nick. And, thank you."

"That's OK," said Nick. "You see, I have a vested interest in that horse you know. If you win at Hawthorn, she'll be quite a valuable asset. Although of course

I'd never sell her," he added, seeing Kate's worried face.

"See you later," he called.

"Yes, see you later, Nick."

Kate did as Nick suggested, and gradually Feather's movements became more fluid. As she reined back for the last time, she felt pleased. They were really beginning to work well together. And tomorrow she would set her mind to practicing their show jumping. Humming contentedly to herself, she made her way back to the stables.

3

A HASTY DECISION

Izzy drew her knees up under her chin and hugged them to her chest. What a miserable weekend it was – the first day of Christmas break and the snow was so deep, she couldn't even ride. Vacantly, she stared out of the bedroom window, watching a robin scratching the ground for food. It seemed as though she'd been there for hours, staring and staring. Midnight would be sold by Friday. There must be a way around it. There must be something she could do to stop him from going to the sale. If only she could find the money to pay for his board herself. But how?

The more Izzy thought about life without Midnight, the more she couldn't bear it. Christmas had seemed so far off in the warmth of the summer days. She had been sure something would come up to stop him from going. But now time had almost run out for them both.

She felt the panic rising in her throat. What would she do without him?

Sliding down from the window seat, Izzy picked up a horsy magazine. She flicked through the pages before throwing it back on the pile it had come from. Maybe she should try talking to her father again one last time.

He was supposed to be going into the city today. She'd make him some lunch before he went, to try and put him in a good mood. Padding across the carpet, she opened her bedroom door and hurried down the stairs.

A grilled cheese sandwich was easy enough. Tiptoeing around the kitchen so as not to disturb him, she gathered what she needed and put the sandwich in the toaster oven. Then she wandered into the living room and picked up the local newspaper from the coffee table.

Pictures with Santa in the Colcott town hall, Christmas bazaar at the Women's Institute, St. Olaf's church jumble sale... there was a lot going on in Colcott at the moment. And then...

Bleeep... bleeep... bleeep... bleeep... bleeep!

Izzy's thoughts were interrupted by a shrill, piercing sound that filled the house. "Oh no-ooo." Izzy shot into the kitchen. The smoke alarm! Her father would be furious.

Cringing, she pulled the tray of charcoaled toast out of the toaster oven. Izzy's father hurried from his study, madly waving a hanky around his head as he tried to ward off the clouds of smoke.

"Izzy, what on earth are you doing?" he bellowed, trying desperately to stop the noise. Izzy held her hands over her ears as she watched him, the high-pitched whistle reverberating around the house.

And then at last he reached up and yanked the battery out of the alarm.

"Phew." Izzy's father looked angry. "I don't believe it. I've got to leave in five minutes and I smell of burned toast," he said, crossly.

"Sorry Dad. I was only–"

But it was too late. Mr. Paterson was already halfway up the stairs, taking two at a time.

Izzy *had* to talk to him before he left.

"Look Dad. There's something I need to say," she started, as he reappeared at the top of the stairs.

"Not now, Izzy," he said, heading down the stairs for the door.

"But Dad. It's about Midnight. I've got to speak to you before it's too late."

"Too late!" Mr. Paterson turned and looked furiously at her. "We've gone over it again and again. The answer's no. Now I've got to go. I'm late as it is," he said, slamming the door behind him.

Izzy hung her head balefully as she heard the car start up. Her mother wouldn't be back for ages either. Ever since she'd started her new job in Colcott she'd hardly been around. It was the third Saturday in a row she'd had to go into the office. Slumping onto the sofa, Izzy put her head in her hands. Slowly, she started leafing through the newspaper in front of her. And then she saw the advertisement. "Hawthorn Horse Trials,

Saturday 11th January. Dressage, cross-country and show jumping," she read out loud. "New junior event for 12 year olds and under. First prize $200."

Izzy wandered off in the direction of the door, clutching the newspaper to her chest. *Hawthorn Horse Trials... $200.*

Stumbling over a chair leg, she kept on reading as she walked up the stairs to her bedroom. Not until the door was closed behind her, did she let out a loud sigh. Her heart was thumping and her mind raced. "Two hundred dollars – that would tide her over, wouldn't it? Surely that would pay for at least a month's board. But the 11th of January was three weeks away and Midnight would have been sold by then.

Thoughtfully, she bit her bottom lip. And then she had an idea. Quick as a flash, she bolted down the stairs and crept into her father's study. Before she had a chance to change her mind, she sat down at the computer and turned it on. Impatiently, she drummed her fingers on the desk as she waited for it to boot up. And then she started typing.

Dear Mrs. Charlwood, she typed, carefully. She took a deep breath, before launching in.

It was very kind of you to offer my daughter, Izzy, your horse, Midnight. She paused for a moment to read what she had written. That sounded good.

As you know, she simply adores him, so it was very hard for me to say no. Unfortunately, my wife and I have been so busy that we didn't think we'd have the time to help her look after him. Now, however, I seem to be able to see a light at the end of the tunnel, and I should have my book finished by Christmas. Izzy's schoolwork seems to have taken a turn for the better and...

At this point Izzy felt the first twinge of guilt. Well, it was only a small lie – her history grades had gone up a little. She went on... *as Christmas is just around the corner I thought it would be nice if Izzy could have Midnight – if that is still all right with you. She told me that he hasn't been sold yet, but is due to go to the Ash Hill Sale on Friday. I tried to call you yesterday to talk things through, but couldn't get hold of you. Izzy was so anxious for it to be cleared up as soon as possible, that I said I would write and let her bring the letter to you in person.*

Izzy didn't stop to read what she had written and continued to type:

Thank you so much for all the kindness you have shown Izzy over the past year and good luck with the big move.

Now, how should she end the letter? Seasons Greetings? No, that sounded silly. Best wishes? No, that was too familiar. In the end, she settled simply for *Yours sincerely*. Quickly she read what she had written. It was perfect. Sneaking a piece of stationery from her father's drawer, she set the computer to print.

"Come on," she muttered, impatiently. With a final roll, the computer had finished its job. Izzy was quick to erase the file and switch off the computer. Snatching the letter, she signed it with a flourish: *Maximillian Paterson.*

Izzy looked at her watch. Two thirty. The sooner

she knew the answer the better. She picked up her jacket from the coat stand. Wrapping a scarf tightly around her neck, she hurried out of the door, grabbed her bike and took off.

Before long, Izzy found herself pedaling up the long, tree-lined drive to Mrs. Charlwood's house. She made her way to the front door and pressed the doorbell.

Rubbing a patch on the window with her glove, she peered into the hall. Boxes and packing cases were stacked high. Patiently, she waited as the bell jangled inside. There was no answer. She felt a twinge of relief. Perhaps there wasn't anyone there after all and she wouldn't have to go through with it. And then she heard someone inside. Mustering up a cheery smile, she rubbed her hands together as the door opened.

"Izzy! What a pleasant surprise," Mrs. Charlwood said. "I didn't expect to see you today. Come in or you'll catch your death out there."

"Oh Mrs. Charlwood, you're not going to believe this." Izzy didn't stop to draw breath, and her words followed one after the other in rapid flow. "I've just had the most fantastic news. It's all in the letter."

"Now, slow down, Izzy." Mrs. Charlwood looked puzzled. "What letter?"

"From my father," Izzy said breathlessly, as she handed it over. "He says I can have Midnight."

"Really? But that's wonderful news. Are you quite sure?" Mrs. Charlwood took the letter eagerly.

Nervously Izzy shifted her weight from one foot to the other as she watched Mrs. Charlwood read.

"I wonder what made your father change his mind," she said, thoughtfully.

Izzy squirmed uncomfortably.

"Oh well," Mrs. Charlwood went on. "Who am I to talk about changing one's mind," she smiled. "If he says you can have Midnight, of course you must. I'll just give your father a call and confirm things with him."

Izzy's head pounded and she felt the blood rising to her head.

"Oh, but you can't Mrs. Charlwood!" The words tumbled out before she had a chance to stop herself.

Mrs. Charlwood looked surprised. And then Izzy relaxed as she remembered there wasn't anyone at home.

"I mean... I mean... when I left, Dad was just on his way into the city for a business meeting."

Mrs. Charlwood thought long and hard. "Well, I suppose I can call him later. You and I can decide where to keep him, can't we?"

"Yes, yes." Izzy smiled and exhaled slowly. For the time being, she'd gotten away with it, and she'd just have to intercept any phone calls later. Hopefully Mrs. Charlwood might forget to call, what with the move and everything.

"Now," Mrs. Charlwood started. "Where does your father want you to keep him?"

Izzy hesitated. She hardly dared breathe. "Oh he said I should work something out with you."

"Hmm. Well, let me see. Do you know of anywhere around here?"

"Well no," Izzy said, shaking her head.

"What about that stables where you rode before you met Midnight?"

"The Elm Park Riding Stables? Well–" Izzy hesitated. It was the last place in the world she wanted to send Midnight. No, that would never do – all those terrible girls interfering in her business. It was best to steer clear of them.

"Well, what about Sandy Lane Stables over by Ash Hill? Have you heard of it?" Mrs. Charlwood said.

"I don't think so," said Izzy.

"It's got a very good reputation," said Mrs. Charlwood. "I know Nick Brooks who owns it, although I haven't seen him for a while. He's a superb rider... taught my Jane to ride... he used to rent a room from us. He was a top steeplechase jockey you know. Jane had lost her nerve after a bad fall and well... Nick managed to restore her confidence in horses – marvelous really. He got married a few years ago and set up Sandy Lane. I don't know his wife, but I'm sure she must be nice for Nick to have married her," Mrs. Charlwood rambled on. "So you could think about sending Midnight there."

"Well, it sounds perfect," Izzy said aloud, silently thinking about the practicalities of it all. The Hawthorn Horse Trials weren't until the 11th January, so she wouldn't be able to pay for his board right away, if at all. Suddenly the craziness of her scheme struck Izzy. What had she been thinking? She and Midnight worked well together, but there was no guarantee they'd win. But Mrs. Charlwood was going on now about how wonderful Sandy Lane was and how happy Midnight would be there. Midnight! At the sound of his name, Izzy was brought to her senses. She had to think fast.

"There is just one small problem, Mrs. Charlwood," Izzy mumbled, shiftily. "Dad did say that he wouldn't be able to pay board at a stables until the end of January when he gets paid for his book."

"Oh dear," Mrs. Charlwood looked thoughtful. "Well that might be a bit more of a problem–" she broke off. "Let me see what I can do. I'll call Nick right now and ask him about it."

"Thanks," Izzy said gratefully, blushing furiously.

"I won't be a minute," Mrs. Charlwood said, hurrying off down the hallway. "Why don't you go and see Midnight? I'll meet you by his stall."

"OK," Izzy said, and hurriedly she made her way into the stables, her feet crunching through the snow. She felt sick with herself. How could she have been so dishonest? And with Mrs. Charlwood of all people. How could she have lied like that? It wasn't too late to turn back and tell the whole truth.

As Izzy turned the corner into the stables, she saw Midnight looking out over his stall door. He whinnied loudly at her approach. No, it was too late. She simply couldn't turn back – not now. She couldn't give him up. Fishing around in her pocket, she pulled out a stray sugar cube and offered it to the black horse.

"Here you are Midnight," she crooned as he nuzzled into her hand.

"That's all settled," a voice called from behind her. Izzy turned around quickly. It was Mrs. Charlwood.

"Nick says you can pay at the end of the month – as long as you don't forget or anything," she joked easily.

Izzy blushed furiously.

"Not that that's going to happen of course," Mrs. Charlwood laughed. "Anyway, Nick's delighted to be getting you both. So I'll arrange for Midnight to be trailered over as soon as possible. No, don't worry about the cost." She held up her hand as Izzy opened her mouth to speak. "It's really the least I can do," she said. "I never felt happy about leaving him to go to the sale without me, so you could say you're sort of doing me a favor too. Anyway, enough of all that. I've got to get back to my packing and I expect you'll want to share your news with the old boy anyway," she said, a twinkle in her eye.

"I'm going to miss you, Midnight." Mrs. Charlwood reached up to pat the black horse's neck, tenderly pulling the scraggly hair between his ears. "But Izzy's going to be looking after you from now on, and you couldn't ask for a better owner, could you?" Mrs. Charlwood turned and smiled at Izzy, not seeming to notice her red face.

"One more thing," she called, looking back. "I just want to let you know how pleased I am. In fact," she paused, "you've made my day. I'd rather he went to you than anyone else."

Izzy stood outside Midnight's stall, silently watching Mrs. Charlwood hurrying off. She felt awful. Midnight was hers, and yet she suddenly felt as though she had the weight of the whole world on her shoulders. Uncertainly she turned for home, sneezing as soft flakes of snow began to settle on her jacket.

4

A NEW ARRIVAL

"Come on, gather around everyone," Nick called across the yard. "There are things we need to discuss."

Kate looked up from where she was sweeping and hurried over to join the others. As Nick ran through the list, she leaned on her broom and listened.

"So, we won't be giving any lessons on Christmas or the day after," he said.

"Then who's going to muck out and exercise the horses?" Charlie asked.

"Sarah and I can cope with that, but if you have any spare time to come and help out, that would be great," Nick started. "And there's something else too – you'll be pleased to hear that we've got a new horse arriving at Sandy Lane this afternoon."

There were low murmurings as everyone started talking amongst themselves.

"He was booked in a few days ago," Nick went on.

"Whose is he?" Tom asked.

"Well," Nick hesitated. "He belongs to an old friend of mine – a Mrs. Charlwood – and she's given the horse away to–"

"GIVEN him away?" Kate burst out, tucking a strand of blonde hair behind her ear.

"Don't look so shocked," Nick laughed. "He was her daughter, Jane's, horse, and Jane's grown up now... moved to Australia... has a baby of her own to look after. Mrs. Charlwood's emigrating to join her. So she's given him to the girl who's been looking after him for the last year – Izzy Paterson. Do any of you know her?"

The riders all looked blankly at each other and shook their heads.

"Should we know her?" Tom asked.

"Well, she lives in Colcott, so she must go to school around here," Nick mused. "She's about your age, Kate," he went on.

"Well, she's not in my class at school," Kate said, shaking her head thoughtfully. "Hmm, Izzy Paterson. I wonder what she's like."

"Anyone Mrs. Charlwood thinks is OK to give Midnight to must be pretty special in my eyes," Nick went on. "He's an amazing show jumper. Jane won lots of prizes with him. It'll be good to have some new talent at the stables and since he's only being kept on at half-board, so we'll be able to use him in lessons."

"And is this Izzy an amazing rider too?" Kate heard

Tom asking in a concerned voice.

"Worried about the competition are you, Tom?" Charlie teased.

"No," Tom spluttered, embarrassed. "I was just asking."

"Well, that's where my information dries up, I'm afraid," Nick laughed. "I only know as much as I've told you. You'll just have to wait and see. Now come on everyone, let's get going. We need to get the spare stall ready for him and the noon ride's going out in a minute."

The chattering continued as Kate turned back to Feather's stall. It didn't take her long to tack up the little gray Arab and soon she was leading her out of the stables.

"Let's go before we freeze on the spot," Nick's wife, Sarah, called from where she was standing with Storm Cloud. "All set to ride to the lighthouse?"

"Yes," a chorus of voices answered.

"Right, come on then," Sarah called, heading into the icy wind.

As they trotted down the bumpy lane, Kate looked around at all of her friends. Jess and Rosie were inseparable, Alex and Tom had been best friends for years and Charlie – well Charlie just fit in anywhere. But what about her? Kate was acutely aware that she was the youngest of the group, and although none of them actually ever said anything, she did feel a little out of things at times. Maybe this new girl would be a friend for her.

"Come on Kate, wake up," Sarah called.

"Coming Sarah."

Kate nudged Feather on into a trot and they approached Sandy Lane Cove.

"We're going to have a canter," Sarah called, drawing to a halt at the top of the cliffs, and looking down at the swirling mass of sea below them. "Take it easy."

Kate followed on behind the others at the back of the string and one by one the riders streamed forward. The little gray horse's hooves drummed along the hard ground and they flew across the turf. Kate's face felt cold. She bent her head low to shield herself from the coastal wind and felt a surge of adrenalin rushing through her.

"Hurray," she whooped as they reached the corner of the fields. Nothing could match riding. As they wound their way around the coastal path and through Larkfield Copse, Kate felt content. Lazily, she stretched her legs out of the stirrups, patiently waiting for Sarah to open the iron gate to the furrowed fields beyond. One by one the riders made their way back to the stables. As they clattered into the stable yard, Nick was waiting for them.

"He's here," he said proudly, leading a black horse out of a stall.

The horse arched his neck and blew softly through his nostrils. As he walked forward, he nuzzled Nick's hand. He was magnificent. Jet-black from head to toe with just the tiniest sprinklings of white hairs forming a star on his forehead.

"He's just as I remembered him," Nick said.

"What's his name?" Kate asked.

"Well," Nick laughed. "It's kind of a long story really. He's registered under the name of Firebird, but I've always just known him as the Midnight Horse." Nick stopped for a moment, a wry grin spreading across his face as he looked at the puzzled faces waiting for an explanation.

"I was living at the Charlwoods when I first met him," he started. "I was a steeplechase jockey at the time and this boy here was kept out in the fields in the back of the house. He used to gallop around at night, trying to get out, and whenever I asked anyone who he belonged to or why no one ever came to ride him, everyone just kept quiet – that's when I first started calling him the Midnight Horse. Later I found out that the Charlwood's daughter, Jane, had lost her nerve in an accident and wouldn't ride any more. So I decided I'd get Jane to ride again... and I did."

Nick smiled at his fond memories. "The Midnight Horse sort of just stuck... then it got shortened to Midnight. Mrs. Charlwood always said she hoped she'd never have to sell him," he went on, patting the horse's shoulder fondly. "And I suppose in a way she hasn't."

Lucky Jane Charlwood, Kate thought to herself, and more importantly now, lucky Izzy Paterson. Her eyes followed the black horse as Nick led him around the yard. Yes, the name Midnight just suited him.

"Did Izzy come with him, Nick?" Sarah called across the stable yard.

"No, he was just delivered. I'm sure she'll be along later though," he started. "Anyway, let's get back to work," he said, as Kate stood tracing her foot in the gravel.

"I'd love to ride him," Kate started.

"Well I don't see why you shouldn't. Why not try him in the 10 o'clock ride on Friday?" Nick offered.

"Really?" Kate was flabbergasted.

"Really," Nick smiled. "But only if his owner doesn't have plans to ride him then herself."

"Excellent," Kate answered, rushing off to Feather's stall before Nick could change his mind.

As she grabbed a body brush, she took another look at the horse, his head silhouetted against the door frame. He was truly beautiful. She wondered why his owner hadn't come. She certainly couldn't love him very much if she could leave him by himself for any length of time. As she returned his gaze, Midnight whinnied loudly. Kate walked back across the stable yard and gave him a reassuring pat.

"Don't you worry," she said. "I'll look after you. You won't be so lonely with me around."

"Are you going to be long, Kate?" Alex called over to her.

"Probably about another half an hour," she answered.

"OK, well I won't bother waiting for you then," Alex said. "Remember we've got that carol service with Mom and Dad tonight and Granny and Grandpa are arriving too."

"OK, Alex," Kate answered. "I won't be long."

"Good-night everyone," Alex called to all his friends. "Merry Christmas." His voice reverberated around the stables as five friendly faces looked up from their tasks.

"Yes, have a good Christmas, Alex," a chorus of voices returned.

5

THE MIDNIGHT HORSE

Christmas passed in a whirl of excitement. Kate got a
beautiful pair of leather riding gloves from Alex, which
made her glad she had spent all that extra money on
his riding crop. Everyone was in high spirits – singing
carols, eating far too much, playing games... the day
was over all too soon.

"How was Christmas, Kate?" Nick called as she
rode her bike into the stable yard two days later.

"Great," she answered. "I got some riding gloves
from Alex and a new jacket from Mom and Dad, but
after the amount I ate, I'll have problems getting into
it! Where are the others?"

"Not sure," Nick answered.

"Alex won't be here till later. He's gone to the
Christmas sales at the mall with Mom. She wants to
buy him a winter coat. How's Midnight?" she asked.

"Fine," Nick called.

"And what about his owner?" Kate asked slowly.

"Hasn't turned up yet," Nick answered.

Kate breathed a sigh of relief. With any luck, she'd still be able to ride him in the 10 o'clock ride.

"I don't even have a number to call to see where she is and Mrs. Charlwood's already left the country," Nick went on. "I suppose I should check the phone book."

Kate followed Nick into the tack room where he picked up the phone book and started flicking through the pages. "Patching, Pater, Paton," he muttered, running his finger down the list. "Well, so much for that idea," he said. "There are no Patersons listed in Colcott. They must be unlisted."

"So does that mean I can ride him in the 10 o'clock?" Kate asked anxiously.

"All right then," Nick grinned. "Go and get tacked up."

Kate didn't need a second invitation. Running across the stables, she drew back the bolt to Midnight's stall and ran a hand down his sleek, polished neck.

"OK, boy," she grinned. The black horse snorted. Kate leaned against his shoulder, lifting each of his hooves to pick them out. His head nodded contentedly as she groomed him quickly and then led him over to the group of riders who stood chattering. She felt pleased as she noted their admiring expressions.

"Where'd he come from? I haven't seen him before, Kate," one of them called.

"He's new at the stables," Kate answered. "He's called Midnight. Isn't he beautiful?" she said, putting her foot into the stirrup iron and springing lightly into the saddle. "He was delivered on Christmas Eve." She patted his sleek neck and gathered up the reins.

"Who does he belong to?" the other girl asked.

"A girl called Izzy Paterson, but she hasn't shown up yet," Kate answered.

"All ready?" Nick called, walking forward on Whispering Silver. He looked around him at the group of riders. "Let's go," he said, turning out of the stable and down the driveway. As Kate followed behind them, she saw Sarah standing at the door to the house and waved.

"He's lovely," Sarah said.

"Isn't he?" Kate answered, happily. As they clattered out of the stable grounds, Kate settled down to his long, easy stride.

"Trot on," Nick called.

One by one the riders kicked their mounts forward. Kate squeezed her calves very lightly and Midnight went into a trot. He was wonderful to ride. Kate looked around her at the surrounding countryside. The snow had already melted, leaving a sludgy brown mud behind. Kate was sad to see the snow go. Still, at least it meant they could go out riding again. As the riders slowed their pace back down to a walk, the ponies' breaths came short and sharp in the crisp winter air.

Nick drew to a halt and jumped to the ground to open the gate to Bucknell Woods. The ground was churned in furrows where a tractor had left its mark. The horses picked their way into the woods. The smell of the pine trees engulfed Kate and she took a gulp of air. Then they were off again.

Kate sat tight to the saddle as they cantered through the trees and popped over a fallen log. Drawing to a halt by a little clearing of trees, Kate couldn't think of anywhere she would rather be than out riding Midnight. She looked at her watch – there was still another hour to go... wonderful!

****

"Atishooo!" Izzy Paterson sat up as her mother pushed open the door to her bedroom, carrying a mug.

"Here Izzy. Drink this," she said.

Izzy groaned, feeling rotten as her head slumped back onto the pillow. "I'm starting to feel a little better now. I should be able to get up later," she said, unconvincingly.

Mrs. Paterson frowned. "I don't think you will, Izzy," she said. "Remember what Dr. Buxton said."

Izzy grimaced as she sat up to take the mug, remembering only too well what Dr. Buxton had said.

"A bad case of flu. Stay in bed and rest for at least a week." Those had been his exact words. He had looked down her throat, listened to her chest and finally made his pronouncement. She hoped Midnight didn't think she had abandoned him. Izzy took a sip from the steaming mug and closed her eyes. She felt so helpless just lying there.

"What's bothering you, Izzy?" Mrs. Paterson asked. "You're not still upset about that horse are you?"

"No," Izzy said, a wave of guilt flooding through her.

"Well, if it's because you're missing this evening at your cousins', then you don't need to worry. I'll get them to come and visit you next week."

"Oh Mom, that's the last thing I want," Izzy moaned, rolling onto her side. "You know I've got nothing in common with Holly and Melanie. I hate talking about clothes and they think I'm crazy when I talk about horses."

How could she tell her mother the real reason for her anxiety – that this was the fourth day away from a horse she wasn't even supposed to have? Izzy stared miserably out of the window.

Izzy's mother sighed. "You will be all right here on your own, won't you?"

Izzy nodded.

"Mrs. Watson from next door said she'll come and check on you in half an hour, and we won't be long."

"OK Mom," Izzy said. Mrs. Paterson closed the door behind her.

Izzy sighed. She so wanted to see Midnight, but she'd just have to wait until Mrs. Watson came and went before she could even think about doing anything. Izzy lay very still, patiently waiting for what seemed like ages.

At last Mrs. Watson arrived and made her another hot drink, fussing around her like a mother hen. It wasn't until she was ready to go that Izzy started to feel a little better.

"I'll leave you now, Izzy," Mrs. Watson said kindly. "You must be tired."

Izzy nodded, feeling guilty that she hadn't made any effort at conversation. Still, she had to get a move on. Izzy waited till she heard the door slam. Then, quickly, she struggled out of bed and into her clothes.

Feeling giddy as she made her way down the stairs, she reached for the key. She grabbed her father's big overcoat and shut the door behind her before hurrying over to her bike. She'd have to be quick, as Sandy Lane was a good ten minute bike ride away over on the other side of Ash Hill. She knew she wasn't really up to it, but she just had to see Midnight. Swaying as she turned the pedals on her bike, she gripped the handle bars tightly and set off down the road.

8 o'clock. The cold night air sent a chill running through her body and Izzy shivered. It wasn't a long way, but it seemed to take forever as she pedaled down the dark country lanes. She turned down Sandy Lane and then she saw the sign for the stables and swung into the driveway.

All was quiet as she propped her bike up by a water trough and looked around her. Luckily, no one was around. Quietly, she glanced into the first stall. Not there.

And then she heard a loud whinny – a whinny she instantly recognized. Midnight! Spinning around she saw the black horse's familiar face looking out over a stall door.

"Ssh my boy," she said, rushing over. "You'll wake up the whole neighborhood." She drew back the bolt and stepped inside.

"I can't stay with you long, Midnight," she said, burying her head in his mane. "I'm not even supposed to be out, but I just had to see you. Don't worry, I'll be back soon. After all, we've got a lot of work to do if we're going to be fit for Hawthorn," she wheezed. "I feel awful and I'm going to have to leave you, but I'll be back again tomorrow to see you."

The horse whinnied softly as Izzy turned to go. Shivering in the cold air, she set off back down the roads she had just ridden along no more than a quarter of an hour ago. She hadn't had long with Midnight, and she felt even worse than when she had left the house, but at least she had seen him – that made all the difference. And surely she would feel better tomorrow.

6

ANOTHER COMPETITOR

Unfortunately for Izzy, she didn't feel any better the next day, or the next. Going out in the cold night air had set her back, and it wasn't until Monday that she was allowed out. As she rode along the winding roads to Sandy Lane, Izzy felt nervous at the prospect of turning up at the stables... more nervous than she had felt about anything in a long time.

"Just go along, Izzy," Mrs. Charlwood had said, "You'll be fine. Nick will look after you."

It had all sounded so easy in theory, but now that Izzy was on her way there, now that Mrs. Charlwood was on the other side of the world, Izzy didn't feel quite so confident.

"Be calm, be sure of yourself, march in briskly," she told herself. But as she jumped off her bike by the water trough and stared into the stable yard, calm and sure of herself was the last thing Izzy felt.

She looked around her. The stables looked busy. People were running around chattering excitedly, laughing and joking. All Izzy wanted to do was turn around and creep away. Nervously, she shifted her weight from one foot to the other as she thought about what to say. She took a deep breath and, although she felt as though her heart might leap out of her skin, she walked into the stable yard.

****

Kate didn't see Izzy hesitating at the end of the row of stalls. She was too busy with Midnight. This was the fourth day she had been looking after him and he was already beginning to recognize her. As she groomed him, she let her mind replay the last few days. Nick had been right. He really was a dream to ride.

"OK boy?" Kate said, patting his black neck. "I'll just get you tacked up."

As she crossed the stable yard to get his saddle, Kate saw a girl walking towards her.

"Hello. Can I help you?" she asked, politely.

"Possibly," the girl answered. "I'm looking for Nick Brooks. You don't happen to know where I'll find him, do you?"

"Yes, he's in the house," Kate answered.

"Oh, OK. Look, I'm Izzy Paterson," the girl started.

"Oh... we've been expecting you since Christmas Eve." Kate stared, her mind in a whirl.

"Well, I've been sick in bed. I've had the flu," Izzy said, gruffly. "Look, where's my horse?"

She spoke so sharply and didn't even smile. Kate took an instant dislike to her.

"I'll take you to him," she said, quickly.

A stilted silence hung in the air. For a brief moment, the two girls stood frowning at each other, and then Kate recovered her manners.

"He's over here," she said, clearing her throat.

Midnight nickered softly as Izzy and Kate hurried over to him. Kate drew back the bolt to his stall and stood back as Izzy rushed in. The horse whinnied in recognition.

"Silly old boy," Izzy crooned.

Kate looked on enviously, feeling strangely distant as she watched the exchange. She turned away sadly, intending to go and get Nick, but just at that moment, he came into view.

"Nick, Izzy Paterson's arrived," Kate called.

Nick hurried over to the stall. "Hello, I'm Nick Brooks," he said, looking in. Kate hung back, watching.

"Hi," the girl answered. "I'm sorry I didn't come before, but I couldn't. You see, I've been sick."

"Well don't worry. Kate's been taking good care of Midnight," Nick said. "But if you could give me your phone number, I can put it up on the tack room notice board with all the others."

"Oh, I can't," Izzy answered sharply, and then she bit her tongue as she saw Nick's surprised face. "Look, it's my Dad," she explained quickly. "He's a writer. He doesn't like being disturbed. He won't let anyone have our number. I'm sorry, but that's just the way it is."

Nick frowned. "Well, I do need all of our owners' numbers," he said firmly.

"Um." Izzy hesitated as Nick held out a pad of paper.

"I won't use it unless it's a real emergency," Nick said, persuasively.

"Oh I guess that's OK then," she said, rather reluctantly.

"There's a ride going out at 10 o'clock if you'd like to join it," Nick continued.

"Great," Izzy said, hurrying away without a second glance.

What a rude girl. How could anyone talk so sharply to Nick. There was something decidedly shifty about Izzy Paterson, Kate thought to herself, and she didn't like it one bit. To top it all off, she had been hoping to ride Midnight in that very ride. Hurrying off to find Alex, she bit her lip to hide her disappointment. Alex was in Hector's stall – just where Kate expected to find him.

"She's arrived," Kate called inside.

"Who?" Alex answered, looking puzzled.

"Midnight's owner – Izzy Paterson," Kate answered. "She's finally made it."

"Oh, I'd forgotten all about her. What's she like?"

he asked, a flicker of interest crossing his face.

"Oh I don't know," said Kate. "Kind of a spoiled brat I think. You should have heard the way she spoke to Nick. She made some excuse about how she's been sick with the flu."

Alex laughed. "Well maybe she has. Come on, Kate, give her the benefit of the doubt. Let's go and get ready for the ride."

"I was going to ride Midnight in that ride, and now I can't," Kate said indignantly. She could hear the petulance in her voice, but was powerless to stop it. "Who does she think she is just strolling in here?"

"The owner?" Alex said, good-naturedly.

"What was that, Alex?" Kate asked.

"Nothing," said Alex. "Come on. Let's go."

"All right, all right, I'm coming," Kate said, crossly. She hurried off to get Feather ready. The line of horses were circling the stables as Kate led the gray horse out of her stall and headed off through the back gate. Kate watched Izzy's every move as they rode through the fields. She looked like a real natural. Midnight was perfectly on the bit and Izzy's seat looked just right.

"How long have you been riding, Izzy?" Kate asked, taking Feather up alongside her.

"Well." Izzy paused to draw breath. "Only properly this last year – since I've had Midnight really," she answered. "But I've had lessons on and off for the last five years, although it's not really the same as having your own horse, you know," she babbled.

"I guess not," Kate said, enviously wondering what it would be like to have a horse of her own.

"OK, let's canter over the log," Nick called from the front, disturbing Kate's thoughts.

One by one, the riders turned their horses and took them over the fallen tree trunk. Kate spurred Feather on and the little gray mare responded willingly, soaring over the jump.

As they rode through Larkfield Copse, Kate started to relax. Cantering across the grassy scrub, they drew to a halt at the top of the cliffs. Kate stared at the beach below. It was deserted, the wind whipping up the waves until they crashed against the shore. Slowly, the string of horses made its way down the cliff path and the blustery wind swept past Kate, carrying words in snatches from Nick's mouth.

"Kate's the only one entered... two weeks away." Kate's heart started to beat faster. It sounded as if they were talking about Hawthorn. Nudging Feather forwards, she trotted down the hill and neared the leaders, overtaking Alex on the way.

"Hey, keep back, Kate," Alex said testily. "You'll push Tom and me off the path if you're not careful."

"Sorry Alex," Kate said. "I just wanted to ask Nick something."

"Can't it wait until we're on the beach?" Tom added sharply as Chancey jogged forward. But Kate didn't listen. Her eyes were firmly fixed ahead of her. She was now within earshot of Izzy and Nick.

"I've been training Kate for a couple of months now, but it would be great to have another Sandy Lane representative."

Kate's heart skipped a beat. *Another Sandy Lane*

representative? What did Nick mean?

"Oh you've caught up with us, Kate," Nick said, turning in the saddle to face her. "I was just telling Izzy that you're entered for Hawthorn. Izzy's entered too, so you can both train together."

Kate's smile froze on her face. Someone else from Sandy Lane entered for Hawthorn? But it was supposed to be *her* chance to prove herself at Sandy Lane. And here was Izzy, hardly five minutes at Sandy Lane, and already muscling in. Kate couldn't bear the idea of sharing Hawthorn with anyone, and suddenly she felt a cloud of gloom descend upon her. She yearned to ride fast, to speed off and immerse herself in her riding, to forget what she had heard. Kate bit her lip to fight back the tears. She hung back, waiting for the others to go off first. Pulling at Feather's head, she circled the little gray horse who was struggling against her reins. And then Kate released her and urged her forward.

"Come on. Let's go," Kate cried. Water streamed from her eyes and they raced faster and faster. As they battled with the wind, all Kate could hear was the pounding of Feather's hooves. Slowing up to join the group, Kate felt a little better. Riding always did that for her and suddenly she felt more determined... more determined than ever to be the best. She'd just have to make sure she won at Hawthorn.

7

SETTLING IN

Izzy didn't know why she'd been so nervous about turning up at Sandy Lane. It had all been so straightforward. She'd even managed to convince her parents she was just helping out at a local riding stables. All was going according to plan.

Everyone at Sandy Lane had been so friendly – well everyone except Kate. Izzy wasn't sure what the problem was, but ever since Hawthorn had been mentioned, Kate had been really cool and off-hand. Still, she couldn't let that get to her. There were more important things to worry about – like the jumping lesson they were about to start in the outdoor ring. With Hawthorn just a week and a half away, she and Midnight were going to need all the practice they could get.

Quickly, Izzy hurried into Midnight's stall and began to tack him up.

"Come on, breathe in," she whispered. "You're putting on weight. It must be all those extra oats I've been feeding you."

Quickly, she led him out of his stall to join the others. Kate was busy tightening Feather's girth and Tom was already in Chancey's saddle. Alex was leading Hector around and Charlie was ambling around on Napoleon. They were all chatting about their plans. It was New Year's Eve and everyone was excited. Tom was having them all over to his house that evening. Izzy was glad to be included. She was really starting to feel like a part of it all.

"Well, who else are we waiting for?" Nick called, tapping his riding boots impatiently with his crop.

"Me," Jess cried, diving into the tack room.

"And me," Rosie shouted, climbing into Pepper's saddle.

"Meet you at the outdoor ring then," Nick said.

And before any of them had a chance to answer, Nick had headed off down the driveway. Izzy waited for the others to go on ahead of her before following on behind.

"Let's get warmed up. I've laid out a course for you to try," Nick said cheerfully, pointing to the gaily painted fences in the outdoor ring.

Izzy looked around her. It was a simple figure eight course. The hardest fence was probably the triple, coming so close after the parallel bars, but even so, she didn't think Midnight would have a problem with that. Wait till the others saw what he could do. Izzy was so busy planning her route that she only caught the tail end of what Nick was saying.

"So I propose that Alex tries Napoleon, Charlie rides Feather and Jess and Rosie do a simple swap. Tom can ride Midnight and Izzy can try Chancey. Who does that leave? Ah, Kate, you can ride Hector."

Izzy looked up, startled. "I missed all that, Tom," she whispered. "What's going on?"

"He's switching us all around," Tom whispered back. "Nick worries that we become too used to riding one horse. He thinks we get lazy, so he likes us to try all the others. He's right of course. I know all of Chancey's old tricks."

"Oh." Izzy gulped, suddenly feeling sick with nerves. She hadn't ridden another horse for months. She felt wooden as she jumped to the ground and handed Midnight's reins over to Tom.

"Right, well, let's get started then," Nick called once they had warmed up their mounts. "Tom, you take the lead."

Steadily, Tom turned Midnight to the start and they skimmed over the first two jumps with ease. Tom turned him wide for the staircase, urging him up and over and onto the gate. They cleared that and then the parallel bars, landing lightly before the triple bar. Now there was only the double.

"One, two, three, jump," Izzy muttered to herself as she watched, her eyes glued to her horse. He was over the second part of the double. That was a clear round. Izzy felt a stab of pride at the ripple of applause echoing around the ring.

"That was good Tom," Nick said.

"He's wonderful to ride, Izzy," Tom called over.

"Come on then, Kate, your turn," Nick called.

Kate picked up her reins and urged Hector on to the first, taking him around the course at a lumbering pace. Still, she jumped clear.

Izzy felt her nerves tightening as, one by one, Nick called the next name and the next and the next and each of the riders took their turn. The better the others rode, the more nervous Izzy felt. Her palms were clammy as she gripped the reins. If Chancey sensed how nervous she was, he'd be sure to start acting up. The waiting was almost too much to bear and Chancey was working himself up as he pawed the ground.

"Just give him a pat to calm him, Izzy," Tom called. "He hates being kept waiting. Oh, and a quick tip – try not to check his stride before you take off. He doesn't need much lead."

"OK," Izzy answered, trying to sound calm. But Tom's words of advice were actually having the opposite effect and making her feel more nervous. She didn't know how she would manage to get around. As she watched Jess draw to a halt by the group, with one fence down, she realized that Nick was calling her name.

"Izzy, Izzy, can you hear me?"

"Sorry." Izzy blushed furiously. She circled Chancey at a canter and began the course. She was so concerned with trying to get Chancey to look at the jump that she completely forgot Tom's words of advice. Chancey flung his head high into the air and they took off too early. Izzy had completely misjudged it and found herself hanging in mid-air. She hit the saddle with an ungainly thud.

Gritting her teeth, she rode on and placed Chancey at the sharks' teeth. They jumped that clear and turned to the staircase, but Chancey was fighting her every step of the way and Izzy wasn't enjoying it one bit. The chestnut horse seemed to realize it, and he tore forward, cutting corners and heading out of control. Izzy felt as though her arms were being torn out of their sockets as they clipped the staircase and rode at the gate. She felt flustered, her confidence evaporating at every turn. She knew she hadn't given Chancey enough time to look at the jump and he skidded to a halt, his heels digging firmly into the ground. First refusal. Izzy felt herself going bright red as she turned him for a second attempt. Anxious to get on and over she hurried him and again he refused.

"I don't think he's going over that today, Izzy," Nick called kindly. "Try him at the parallel."

Trying to keep her head, Izzy rode him over the parallel and went on to jump the triple bar before heading for the double. One, two and they were over. But by the time they had finished, Izzy's nerves were in pieces.

"Don't worry," Tom said in an understanding voice as she returned to the group. "He just takes a little getting used to. He did the same thing with me when I first rode him. He gets very fresh if he's kept waiting."

Izzy nodded, her pride severely dented. Typically, Chancey had calmed down now and stood quiet and still. Izzy wanted the ground to swallow her up, and she still had another ten minutes of the lesson to get through.

When at last everyone had taken their turn, Izzy jumped off Chancey and returned him to Tom. As she collected Midnight and led him back to his stall, she felt a wave of panic run through her. What if she rode that badly at Hawthorn? What if she couldn't manage it? Once again she felt under pressure. If she didn't win at Hawthorn, she wouldn't even be able to pay what she owed.

"Oh Midnight," she cried, alone in his stall. "Whatever am I going to do?" She jumped as a face appeared over the stall door. It was Kate.

"Did you want something?" Izzy asked, annoyed at herself for voicing her fears out loud when anyone could have heard her.

"I just wanted to check to see if Midnight was OK," Kate answered. "It's getting dark and you seemed to have been in there forever."

"He's fine," Izzy answered, tersely. "Just fine."

"OK. Well, I'm going. I'll see you at Tom's maybe," Kate said, striding away.

8

RIVALS

New Year's Day turned out to be dark and gloomy. Not a good start to the year, Kate thought to herself as she sat alone in the tack room. The sky looked tumultuous and forbidding, black clouds scudding back and forth. Still, yesterday evening had been fun. She rubbed her eyes, finding it hard to stay awake after the late night festivities.

Kate put some saddle soap on her sponge and cast her mind back over the last few days. She and Izzy were training with Nick over the cross-country course that afternoon, and Kate didn't feel much like going out with her at all. Izzy was so prickly and standoffish.

For a brief second, Kate's thoughts were interrupted by the sound of a bicycle skidding to a halt outside. She rose to her feet and looked out of the tack room window. It was Izzy. Just the last person she wanted to see. The others were all out on a ride – she'd have to make polite conversation with her. Kate shifted uncomfortably on her stool as the tack room door swung open.

"Oh, it's you Kate, I didn't realize you were here," Izzy said. "You made me jump. Where is everyone?"

"Sarah's in the cottage," Kate answered, noncommitally, "and the others are out on the 2 o'clock ride. Nick said to clean Feather's saddle before the cross-country this afternoon."

"I should do Midnight's then," Izzy said. "I guess I'll join you."

An uncomfortable silence filled the room as the two girls sat, furiously polishing away at their tack.

"What time did Nick say he'd take us out?" Izzy said at last.

"Three," Kate answered, not looking up.

"Well, it's ten to," Izzy said, looking at her watch. "I think I'd better go and get Midnight ready."

"OK," Kate answered, staying firmly in her seat.

Kate felt relieved to hear the sound of voices outside and jumped awkwardly to her feet.

"Ready to go out over the cross-country course you two?" Nick called across the stable yard.

"Just about," Kate answered.

Hurriedly, she made her way to Feather's stall and tacked up the gray mare. Leading her outside, she headed off to the cross-country course. The course wasn't difficult. There certainly wasn't the variety of jumps there would be at Hawthorn, but it would be good practice all the same. Kate trotted around to warm Feather up and eventually she heard voices. She felt annoyed to see Izzy and Nick chatting so easily together as they ambled through the gate. Quickly, she rode over to meet them.

"We ought to get started," Nick said to the two girls. "The light's already fading. It'll be dark before we know it. Now, remember to ride carefully out there. It's still very slippery and I don't want you breaking your necks."

"OK," Kate answered, her eyes glued to the course ahead of her.

"Why don't you go first Kate, while Izzy gets Midnight warmed up?" Nick suggested.

Kate nodded and nudged Feather on for the brush. Lightly they thundered across the dirt, over the hayrack, before galloping on. They flew over the hedge and into the woods as if they were point-to-point racing. They were going fast... too fast. But something made Kate kick Feather on even more and they raced to the log pile in the trees. Still, Kate didn't slow Feather's pace. The gray horse hurtled forward at breakneck speed, straining at the bit. Clear of the tires, they turned to take the zigzag rails in their stride. Up the hill and over the low gate, they raced, pounding forward for the stone wall.

Feather's sides were heaving in and out like bellows as she cleared the last jump with inches to spare and sprinted back to Nick and Izzy. As Kate drew to a halt she felt uneasy. They had gone pretty fast, and deep down Kate knew it hadn't been safe.

"Hmm." Nick didn't look delighted as he looked down at his stopwatch. "That was very quick, Kate," he said. "You must have cut a few corners in the woods to notch up that speed." Kate felt herself blushing, knowing only too well that Nick's words were very true.

"Your turn, Izzy," Nick started.

Izzy nodded, giving Kate a hard stare as she turned toward the first jump. The black horse thundered across the ground. Kate watched, eagle-eyed. Izzy sat tight to the saddle and they flew over the tiger trap and onto the brush. Then they raced over the hay rack and onto the hedge into the trees. Kate held her breath, waiting to catch sight of them again. One, two, three, four. She counted the seconds under her breath. And then Izzy appeared. Ten seconds. That was fast... reckless even, Kate thought as she watched them clear the zigzag rails and thunder over the low gate, up the hill to the stone wall.

Nick looked serious as Izzy drew to a halt beside him. "I don't know what you two are trying to do," he said at last. "You rode like maniacs out there. I might as well not be giving you any advice for all the attention you paid. You should be trying to ride competently, not almost breaking your necks to beat each other," he said in disgust. "I was going to suggest we practice the log pile, but I think we'd better get back to the stables."

"But Nick," said Kate. "You said we could ride until four."

"I think I've seen enough of your riding for one

day, don't you?" he said, sharply. "I suggest you rethink your attitudes if you want me to train either of you any more. Meet me in the tack room tomorrow at nine. I haven't got time to go over things now. Sarah and I are going out for dinner tonight."

And with that, he turned Whispering Silver to the gate, leaving the two girls looking equally sheepish. It was a few moments before either of them spoke and then Izzy was the first to start.

"I suppose he's right, Kate," she said. "We did ride a little too fast out there."

Kate knew only too well that what Izzy was saying was true, but she didn't want to agree with her.

Izzy waited for a few moments, before shrugging her shoulders and turning to the gate.

Well so what? Kate thought to herself. Izzy was no friend of hers. And if she had never turned up at Sandy Lane, Kate would never have had to compete with anyone anyway, would she? Still, as she walked Feather through the gate, Kate couldn't help but feel a little guilty at the way she had ridden. She was well aware that she had been the one who had set the precedent. Perhaps she should say something to clear the air. Kate looked across at Izzy and noted the self-defiant expression on her face. No, it was better to leave things as they were.

"I'm sorry Feather," Kate whispered, as she jumped down outside the barn. "I know I pushed you," she said, leading the little Arab into her stall.

Feather nickered softly as if in response, and Kate picked up the body brush to start work on her coat.

She must have gone over her back for some time because, before she knew it, she was in total darkness. Rushing across the stables, she picked up Feather's haynet.

"Kate," Izzy called tentatively across the stables.

Kate didn't answer, and the voice came again, louder this time. "Kate!"

Kate spun around. What did she want? And then she looked around and saw that no one else was in sight. The others must have gone home.

"Midnight's acting really weird," Izzy called over. "Could you come and look at him?"

"I am in kind of a hurry," Kate answered, coolly. "Well, maybe just a quick look," she said, her curiosity getting the better of her. "What's wrong?"

"Well, he's just really restless. He'll hardly let me go anywhere near him."

Kate looked into the stall. Inside, the horse's head was bent toward the floor and his ears were laid flat back.

Kate was puzzled. She slid back the bolt and slipped inside. Gently, she held out her hand to try to soothe him but Midnight bared his teeth.

"Hmm," she said. "I don't think he's in a very good mood tonight, are you boy?" she said, patting his shoulder. "He's probably just tired – you did push him pretty hard out there."

"Well if you hadn't forced me–" And then Izzy stopped herself and looked embarrassed.

Kate was surprised by the outburst. She had obviously rubbed a raw nerve.

Izzy started again, more calmly this time. "I was just going to try to catch Nick before he goes out," she said. "But I'd feel silly if it's nothing... maybe I'll see how he is in the morning."

Kate shrugged her shoulders and turned away. She was relieved that Izzy had taken the decision out of her hands. She would rather not see Nick again that night anyway.

9

PANIC-STRICKEN

As Kate rode home that evening along the dark, winding lanes, she couldn't stop thinking about Midnight. She'd dismissed Izzy's notion without really thinking about him. What if there was something wrong with the black horse? What if she'd let her irritation with Izzy get in the way of his need? Nick had always said that if anything was wrong with one of the horses, they were to alert him right away.

"Kate, is that you?" she heard her mother calling as she walked in through the back door. "Where have you been? You said you'd be back by four thirty. You know I worry about you cycling home when it's dark."

Kate sighed. "Sorry Mom," she said sheepishly,

putting her head around the kitchen door. "There was something wrong with one of the horses at the stables. And – well, anyway, I'm sorry."

"Hmm, make sure you're not late again," her mother said.

"OK," Kate said, happy to agree to anything, if only to escape the lecture.

"Come and sit down and have your supper. Dad and I are going out in a moment. Where's Alex? Alex, your food's getting cold."

Kate washed her hands in the kitchen sink, scrubbing away at the dirt under her nails, before she sat down to eat.

"Where are you going, Mom?"

"The Bicknells'," her mother said. "We won't be back late."

"OK," Kate said as Alex joined her at the table.

"Alex," she started. I'm sort of worried about Midnight. He was really restless when I left. Izzy really pushed him over the cross-country. He was very tired, and then he wouldn't eat anything and..."

"Not that horse again," Alex groaned. "Leave it alone, Kate. It's none of your business. It's not as though you're even a friend of hers."

"It's not her I'm worried about," Kate snapped. "It's the horse. I couldn't give two hoots about her."

"Well, you've made that clear enough," Alex answered.

"What do you mean?" Kate said, through a mouthful of food.

"Well, you haven't exactly been very nice to her,

have you?"

"Well, she's not *exactly* the nicest person you've ever met, is she?"

"She's not bad," Alex said.

Kate felt herself getting mad "*She's not bad*? She's the worst. She's so conceited. All she cares about is winning at Hawthorn."

"Sounds like someone else I know," Alex said, as Kate got up from the table.

"I didn't expect you to understand, Alex." Kate walked off, tears pricking her eyes. How could he? How could her own brother take the side of a complete stranger?

"What's going on?" Mrs. Hardy asked, walking back into the kitchen.

"Nothing," Kate answered.

"OK," Mrs. Hardy said. "We're going in a minute," she said, as she cleared the plates. "Alex, you're in charge."

"Fine," Alex said, an evil grin spreading across his face. "Did you hear that Kate?"

Kate made a face as Alex went into the living room to watch television.

"I'll leave the number by the telephone," their mother called, shutting the front door behind them. "Bye."

Kate was left sitting at the kitchen table. She couldn't stop thinking about Midnight. What if something was wrong with him? If only she could check. Maybe she should go back to the stables...

"Alex." Kate threw back the door to the living room

and walked in.

"Sssh." He motioned to his lips, his eyes glued to the TV.

"But I need to talk to you." She paced up and down.

"Sit down, Kate," said Alex. "You're in the way."

Kate thought hard. There was no point in waiting for him to listen when he was in this sort of mood. "Look," she said. "I'm going back to the stables to check on Midnight. I won't be long."

"What? You're crazy, Kate." Alex was immediately alert. "I'm in charge, and Mom would go nuts."

"Well she'll never know," Kate said defiantly.

And before Alex could stop her, Kate had rushed out of the house and climbed onto her bike.

"Kate, Kate." Alex's voice cried out as Kate rode away, the beam from her lights marking a path through the night. It really was very dark. She started to pedal faster, down road after road.

It wasn't long before she was turning into Sandy Lane. As she headed up the driveway to the stables, she felt relieved to find that things were quiet. She had been silly, panicking unnecessarily. Of course there wasn't anything wrong.

And then she heard a loud moaning sound that caused her to draw her breath in sharply. Even before she had a chance to investigate, Kate knew it was the sound of an animal in pain, and it was coming from Midnight's stall. A high-pitched whinny filled the air. Kate felt as though someone had punched her in the stomach. Without hesitating, she threw her bike to the ground and rushed across the stable

63

grounds to look in the stall.

Inside the stall, Midnight stood bathed in sweat. The whites of his eyes were rolling viciously and the veins on his neck were jutting out like twisted cords. Desperately he lashed out, his hind legs striking the timbered walls behind him with a dull thud. Kate's heart sank. He was sick, desperately sick. Manically he plunged to the ground in sinking motions, his legs buckling beneath him. Up and down... up and down, he reeled.

What should she do? Nick and Sarah were out. Who should she call? She felt scared... scared of what might happen. She had to think straight. "Keep calm, don't panic," she told herself. "Call the vet."

Quickly, she let herself into the tack room and flicked on the light. Slotting a coin into the pay phone, she dialed the vet's number, impatiently shifting her weight from one foot to the other.

"Come on, hurry and answer," she cried.

"Hello, vet's office." The voice came loud and clear.

"Hello, yes, can I speak to the vet?" Kate asked urgently.

"I'm afraid he's on call," the voice said. "I'm his wife."

"Well, there's trouble at Sandy Lane. One of the horses is really sick and I don't know what to do," Kate cried, the panic rising in her throat. "He's going crazy. He looks as though he's going to kick the stall down."

"Whoa, now slow down," the woman answered. "I'll call my husband and get him over there as soon as I can. But first you'll have to tell me what the horse is doing so I can give a clear description to my husband. Take a deep breath."

"Well." Kate paused for a moment, not knowing where to start. "He's kicking at the walls and he keeps rolling around on the ground," she said, uncertainly. "And he's making this groaning noise."

"And how long has this been going on?" the vet's wife asked.

"I don't know," Kate wailed. "I've only just gotten here, but his coat is drenched in sweat."

"Have you taken his temperature?"

"I don't know how to do it," Kate cried, feeling useless.

"Don't worry," the woman said. "My husband can do that. It sounds like colic. I'll get him to come to you as soon as he can. I'll phone him on his mobile. He's up at Grange Farm at the moment – on the other side of Walbrook."

Kate looked at her watch. It would take him a good half an hour to get to Sandy Lane from Walbrook. He wouldn't be with her until at least a quarter after eight.

"It's important that you stay calm," the woman started. "Try and put a halter on the horse and keep him from rolling. He could get stuck on his back otherwise and it'll be difficult to get him up."

"OK," Kate said bravely. "Will he be OK?" she asked quietly.

"I hope so," the woman said, uncertainly. "You could put a blanket on him to keep him warm," she said gently. "But that's about the best you can do. He's in a lot of pain at the moment. Imagine if you had very bad stomach ache – well that's what it feels like – the pain comes in waves."

As Kate put the phone down, she felt strangely detached. She couldn't hear any more sounds, and for a moment, she thought that Midnight had stopped – maybe the pain had eased. Quietly she approached the stall and looked in. Midnight didn't even look up as she stood there. What was it the lady had said? *The pain comes in waves.*

"Come on now," Kate crooned, gently drawing back the bolt on his stall so as not to startle him. "I know you're not feeling very well, but I'm here to help you." She held out her hand as she approached his shoulder.

"Here boy, easy does it," she said, hiding the halter behind her back. Kate edged forward and put a blanket over him, but every time she tried to reach up with the halter, he lurched away.

He was getting restless now, looking around as if to bite at his flanks. Ten minutes had passed since Kate had called the vet, another ten might pass before she could get Midnight into the halter. Kate knew in her heart of hearts that there was only one person who could do it. She took one last look at the horse before running to the tack room. Pulling aside the numbers on the board, she looked for Izzy's phone number. There it was.

Nervously, she slotted another coin into the phone and dialed the number, praying that someone would answer.

"Hello." It was Izzy.

"Hello Izzy, it's Kate."

"Hi," Izzy said, in an uncertain voice.

At the sound of Izzy's voice, Kate clammed up. But then she took a deep breath and let the story spill out. At first she didn't think Izzy could have understood because there was deathly silence, but then Kate heard a whimper, like an animal stunned with pain.

"I'll be right there," Izzy whispered, putting the phone down without another word.

Kate paced around outside for a few moments, wondering where to start. She had to get that halter on him. Midnight was lying down when she looked into the stall. As she drew back the bolt, he struggled to his feet, wobbling from side to side.

"Come on now, I know you're in pain, but the vet will be here soon," Kate said gently.

"Easy does it," she whispered, slowly stroking the horse's nose. "No, no," she cried, realizing that his legs were beginning to buckle beneath him.

But it was too late. The horse was on the floor, rolling in acute agony. And that was the state he was in when Izzy arrived at the stables. Kate looked out over the stall door just as Izzy flung her bike to the ground. Kate felt a pang of sympathy at the sight of Izzy's tear-stained face.

"Oh Midnight, you poor, poor thing," Izzy cried, hurrying over. She backed away as the horse struggled to his feet. "How long did the vet say he would be?" she asked. "And what did he say we should do?"

"We've got to get the halter on him and he shouldn't roll," Kate said quickly.

"OK," said Izzy. "Let's do it."

Slowly, Izzy reached up to the horse's neck and, with a competent hand, slid the halter on over his head. "That's the easy part," she said grimly, turning to Kate. "We'll never be able to keep him standing."

"Yes, we will," Kate said, sounding more confident than she felt. "You stand on his left, and I'll stand on his right. OK?"

"Will he die?" Izzy asked quickly.

"I don't know," Kate answered truthfully, not knowing quite what to say.

Izzy was talking to herself now, muttering under her breath. "It's all my fault. How could I have been so stupid? I'll never forgive myself."

"Of course it's not your fault," Kate said calmly. "And anyway, you shouldn't think like that, not until we hear what the vet has to say."

"But where is he?" Izzy cried in a panic, as she looked at her watch. "You said quarter after eight on the phone. It's eight-thirty now."

"I was estimating," Kate said, through gritted teeth, trying to keep her cool. "I don't know how long the case at Grange Farm's going to take him, do I?"

"I'm sorry, I'm sorry," Izzy said quickly. "I'm just panicking, that's all."

It seemed like they'd been talking forever when eventually they heard a car in the distance. Looking out over the stall door, they saw a Land Rover rattle into the yard. The vet jumped out and walked straight over.

"Where are Nick and Sarah?" he asked, taking the

horse's temperature.

"They're out," Kate answered.

"Unfortunate that something like this should happen the one evening they're not around," he grimaced.

The two girls were quiet as they waited for the vet to say something. He looked thoughtful as he tapped the thermometer and got out his stethoscope. Midnight's eyes were flecked white as the vet listened to his chest and abdomen.

"It's a good thing you called me," he said.

"But how did it happen?" Izzy cried.

"Hmm, well often it's a case of exercising heavily on a full stomach. Has he come in from a heavy ride today?"

The two girls looked at each other and didn't say anything.

"Well, what did he have to eat?" the vet went on, not noticing their stricken faces. "Was he given a big feed for instance?" he asked.

"No, just the normal amount," Kate answered.

"It wasn't the normal amount," Izzy blurted out. "I've been giving him extra feed."

"*Have you*?" Kate looked surprised.

"Yes." Izzy looked worried. "And I did ride him really hard." She looked at Kate and then turned back to the vet. "See we're entered for the Hawthorn Horse Trials the weekend after next," she explained. "I thought giving him more food would build up his energy levels."

"Did Nick tell you to do this?" the vet asked, concerned.

"No." Izzy hung her head. "I just thought..."

"It was a silly thing to do, but try not to worry," he said, patting her on the shoulder.

Quickly, the vet pulled out a syringe from his bag and injected something into the horse's neck. "This is a painkiller and muscle relaxant," he explained. "The effects should be pretty quick, but you'll need to keep a close eye on him for the next couple of hours anyway. I'm afraid I'm going to have to go back to Grange Farm in a moment. He should calm down and be more at ease. Can I leave you to watch him?"

"Of course," the two girls answered in unison, and looked at each other.

"Keep him in his stall. Don't give him any food tonight, but make sure he has water and ring my wife immediately if he starts to look distressed again."

The two girls nodded as the vet disappeared out of the yard.

"You really don't need to stay, Kate," Izzy said. "I'll be all right on my own."

"But I'd like to, if you don't mind, Izzy," Kate said hesitantly. "You see, I know it sounds strange, and I know he's your horse, but I do feel partly responsible for what's happened. If I hadn't been so desperate to race you in the cross-country, you might not have pushed him so hard."

"Oh Kate," said Izzy. "We've been so silly, haven't we?"

The two girls looked sheepishly at each other, embarrassed by their admissions. "Then would you mind if I stayed?" Kate asked.

"I'd like it," Izzy answered slowly. "I'd like the company. I know that we haven't been the best of friends, but we could try, couldn't we?"

"I think so, Izzy," Kate said, reddening and turning away. She wasn't very good at this sort of intimacy and felt awkward. She didn't know what to say.

"I'll just go and phone Alex and tell him what's happened," she said, quickly changing the subject. Hurrying into the tack room, she reached for the phone and slotted in a coin. Shifting her weight from one foot to the other, she waited for an answer, twisting the telephone cord in her fingers. Alex wasn't going to be in the best of moods. The phone rang... once, twice, and then a pinched voice answered at the other end.

"Hello."

"Hello Alex. It's me."

"Kate! Where on earth have you been? I've been worried sick."

"Alex, calm down. I'm all right. I'm at the stables. Midnight's really sick. He has colic."

"Colic!"

"Yes colic," Kate answered. "I called the vet. Izzy's here too, but I'm going to stay with her. Are Mom and Dad back?"

"Not yet, but what am I going to say to them when they do get back?"

"Don't worry, I'll be home before then," Kate said slowly, feeling exhausted.

"Well, if you're not, I'll just have to think of something," Alex said kindly.

"Thanks," Kate said gratefully. That was so like Alex. He might be all big-brotherly and patronizing, but when it came down to it, she knew she could count on his support. And besides, anything to do with horses concerned him as much as it did her. Kate hurried out of the tack room and back to the stall. Izzy stood still, patiently comforting Midnight. He looked terrible. His head hung low and his coat was clumped in whorls, but at least he had calmed down.

"How is he?" Kate called, hurrying back to join Izzy.

"Fine," Izzy answered. "The vet was right, it does seem to be easing off."

"He looks exhausted though," Kate answered. "Don't you, boy?" she said, patting his shoulder. "Well, we'd better settle down and watch him," she said. "I don't think he much likes the idea of sharing his stall with us, Izzy," Kate joked.

"No, he doesn't seem to know what to think, does he?" Izzy answered. She took a deep breath. "Thank you for all you've done, Kate," she said.

"That's OK. And actually, there's something I wanted to say to you, Izzy. I'm sorry I was so funny when you first arrived at Sandy Lane. It's just that you were so off-hand, and well, I couldn't bear the idea of someone else entered for Hawthorn too. We didn't get off to a very good start, did we?" she said.

"No, I suppose not," said Izzy. The two girls looked at each other.

"Let's call it a truce," Kate suggested.

"Yes, truce." Izzy smiled and nodded.

The two girls sat down in the straw, keeping a watchful eye on the black horse. And that was how Nick found them when he returned to the stables at almost midnight. They had a lot of explaining to do...

10

A CHANGE OF HEART

"So he's eating OK now, right?" Kate looked across her bedroom to where Izzy lay sprawled across the floor.

"Pretty much," Izzy answered, flicking through the pages of a pony magazine. "I thought he was going to die," she went on. "I'd never have forgiven myself if he had."

It had been three days since the awful evening Kate had discovered Midnight with colic, and he had made a full recovery. Slowly, the two girls were getting to know each other.

Kate had been in serious trouble when her parents had come back to find her not there. Alex had tried to make excuses for her, but they'd rushed out to the stables immediately. The result had been instant grounding. She'd known she'd had it coming, but still it didn't make it any easier being away from Sandy Lane. She had to content herself with a progress report from Izzy and it just wasn't the same as seeing it with her own eyes.

"He finished off all of his hay tonight, Kate," Izzy started. "But how are you doing anyway?"

"OK," Kate answered glumly. "Bored but OK. It's the first time in my life I can safely say I'll be glad to be going back to school tomorrow. I can't believe you didn't get into trouble for being out so late. Your parents must be so much cooler than mine."

Izzy turned a bright shade of red and it was a while before she spoke. "Er, well, actually I didn't tell them I'd been out," she muttered, finally.

"What?" Kate propped herself up onto her elbow and looked across the room.

Izzy took a deep breath. "Well, they never knew I'd left the house. I climbed out of my bedroom window," she said, nonchalantly. "They never even noticed I was gone."

"What!" Kate looked surprised. "I can't believe it."

Izzy shrugged her shoulders. She desperately wanted to get everything off her chest. She wanted to tell Kate the whole story, but she just didn't know how Kate would react. Every time she went to do it, a nagging voice in her head told her that it would spoil things.

Izzy got up and walked across the room. "Look Kate," she started. "There's something I've got to tell you."

"This sounds serious," Kate joked. "Come on, tell me what it is. What dark secret are you hiding?"

"Well, I don't know where to start really," Izzy said, in a shaky voice.

Kate looked startled. "It can't be that bad, can it?"

"It is–" Izzy started speaking uncontrollably fast and in seconds had blurted out the whole sorry story – how she had come to ride Midnight in the first place, how she had had to turn down Mrs. Charlwood's offer and then the plan to keep Midnight.

"So you see, I just have to win at the trials," Izzy went on. "Everything's riding on it. If I don't, I won't be able to pay Nick what I owe him."

Kate was silent for a moment as she took it all in.

"Say something, Kate," Izzy begged.

"I just don't know what to say," Kate stammered. "I can't believe it. I just can't believe you had the nerve to do it. And you haven't told your parents any of this?"

"Are you crazy? Of course I haven't," said Izzy. "Although they know that I'm riding in a horse trials on Saturday."

"Well, who on earth do they think you're riding?" Kate burst out.

"I told them that Mrs. Charlwood had decided to send Midnight to the stables I've been going to, and that I've been picked to ride him," Izzy started.

"And they believed you?" Kate looked astonished.

"It's sort of true, Kate," Izzy pleaded. "The only thing I haven't told them is that I'm supposed to be paying his board."

"Oh so that makes it all OK, right?" Kate said. She

was deeply shocked, but she was already starting to feel a little sorry, as she stared at her friend's pale face. Izzy looked sick with worry, and now that Kate came to think of it, huge dark shadows ringed her eyes.

"But even if you do win at Hawthorn," Kate started, an awful thought having crossed her mind. "It's hardly going to be enough to pay for his board forever, is it?"

"I know... I know that now," Izzy cried. "I just didn't think about it at the time. I just jumped in feet first. I thought I'd be able to figure out a way to earn the rest of the money later, that I'd do a paper route or something. What would you have done?" Izzy asked. "Would you have just sat by and let Midnight be sold?"

"No, but–" Kate looked thoughtful. "Oh, I don't know, we can't even begin to think about that now. We've just got to try to work this out."

Kate stopped for a moment. What *would* she have done though? Deep down she knew she wouldn't have had the guts to do what Izzy had done and for the first time, she felt a stirring, something like admiration, for the girl who sat so boldly in front of her, pouring her heart out.

"So let's get this straight," Kate started again. "Your parents know that you've been coming to Sandy Lane, they just don't know that Midnight's your horse."

"Yes," said Izzy, waiting for Kate to come up with a solution.

"Well." Kate took a deep breath. "If you want my advice, Izzy, I think you should tell your parents before Hawthorn–"

"*Tell my parents?*" Izzy cried. "But I can't, they'll

go berserk."

"Well, they're going to find out sooner or later, aren't they? Wouldn't it be better if you got it off your chest right away before it gets any worse? They'll know what to do," said Kate.

"They'll just make me sell Midnight," Izzy said, mournfully.

"But if you don't tell your parents, and you don't win at Hawthorn, you won't even have the money to pay Nick and Sarah for his board. At least if you tell your parents, they might help you out before you dig yourself in any deeper."

"I know. I know you're right." Izzy hung her head. "But you don't know my parents. It's not going to be that easy."

"Look," Kate said in a reassuring voice. "If you explain it all to them, the way you've explained it to me, they'll have to understand. Yes, they're going to be furious at first, but if you tell them that the prize money from Hawthorn will cover you for a month's board and that you're sure to win, they might soften and pay for the rest of his stabling," Kate said, sounding more confident than she felt.

"Not a chance," Izzy said glumly. "You don't know my parents, Kate—"

"Kate, Kate." A voice boomed up the stairs, drawing their conversation to a close. "Dinner!"

"Rats," Kate said quickly. "You'll have to go. Look, we'll talk about this some other time. Right now I've got to stay in Mom's good books. I don't want to be grounded from Hawthorn too. Think about what I've said. You'll feel much better once you've told them," she said, rising to her feet. "You've got nothing to lose, have you?"

"I suppose not," Izzy said. "No, you're right, Kate," she said with new resolve. "I'll do it."

"Good," Kate answered, leading Izzy down the stairs.

"Promise you won't tell any of the others about all this?" Izzy whispered, turning back to Kate as they headed for the door. "I couldn't stand it if they found out."

"I promise," Kate sighed.

As Izzy stepped outside, Kate's words rang in her ears. *You've got nothing to lose.* Izzy stopped in her tracks. But she had, hadn't she? They might make her sell Midnight. She had everything to lose.

11

AN UNEXPECTED REACTION

A whole school week had gone by since Izzy had had that conversation with Kate, and still she hadn't done anything about telling her parents. There just hadn't been a suitable moment. Now it was Friday evening and Hawthorn was the next day – that really didn't leave much time. Izzy pushed open the back door to her house and stepped into the kitchen. She felt ready to collapse. It had been a long day at school and on top of that, she'd just spent the last couple of hours at Sandy Lane.

Kate had hardly spoken to her all evening. Izzy knew that Kate was upset that she hadn't told her parents yet.

"There's never quite the right time for you is there, Izzy?" Kate had cried in exasperation. "You'll just feel so much better when you've told them. I wish you'd just get on with it."

"Look Kate–" Izzy had started. But she hadn't gotten any further. Nick had overheard the conversation and had asked them what the problem was. That had shut them up. Izzy had ended up promising Kate she would do something about it that evening.

Izzy sighed as she walked down the hallway. The house was quiet and in total darkness. She looked at her watch. Six o'clock. Her mother was probably still at work, but judging from the light streaming out from under the study door, her father was at home. Twice Izzy walked up to the study to rap on the door, only to walk away again. She felt as though she was standing at the edge of a precipice waiting to jump. It was now or never. Boldly, she knocked on the door.

"Come in," her father's voice answered.

Izzy turned the handle. Inside, her father was shrouded in darkness, a table lamp lighting his work.

"What is it Izzy? I'm really busy," he said.

"Could I talk to you for a minute, please Dad?" she said, nervously.

"Is it important?" he asked, not looking up from his computer.

"Well yes," Izzy answered. "Yes it is." She took a deep breath.

Her father held up his hand before she started. "I know what I meant to tell you," he said. "I got a call today from a guy at that stables you've been going to – someone called Nick?"

Izzy's heart began to beat double time. So Nick had found out already. Had Kate told him? She opened her mouth to say something and closed it again. She couldn't think of an excuse.

"I'm sorry Dad. I'm really sorry. I–"

"Sorry?" Mr. Paterson looked bemused. "Whatever for? I kind of liked him actually. He wanted to know if your mother and I wanted tickets to watch you ride at this horse show thing. He seemed really impressed by you... said you were pretty good, Izzy." Mr. Paterson looked up at his daughter. "This is the first time I've heard anyone rave about your abilities since you were in kindergarten!" he laughed. "Aren't you pleased?"

Izzy couldn't bring herself to say anything as her father went on.

"Anyway, I spoke to your mother and we've decided we're going to come and watch and see how you do. Perhaps there's more to this riding lark than we thought. Izzy are you listening?"

But Izzy was miles away. She felt as though she was hearing everything from a distance. She had to tell him before it was too late.

"Dad," she began. "Oh, it's all such a mess. I don't know where to start–"

"What is it now, Izzy?" Mr. Paterson smiled. "Must you always make a mountain out of a molehill?"

"I'm not this time, Dad. Dad, you're not listening to me," Izzy cried. "You're not listening at all. I've lied. I lied to both you and Mom. Mrs. Charlwood didn't send Midnight to Sandy Lane at all – I did." Izzy blurted the words out.

"You did?" Mr. Paterson looked surprised. "What are you talking about Izzy?"

"Well, I didn't let him go to the sale. I couldn't. You see, I thought that if I could win at Hawthorn, I could pay his board for a month, and then... and then..."

"Whoa, now slow down a minute, Izzy," Mr. Paterson's voice was dangerously careful. "Mrs. Charlwood let you do all this?"

"Well, not exactly," Izzy gulped, looking at her father who was ready to blow a fuse. "You see, I told her you'd agreed to it–"

"WHAT!" Mr. Paterson bellowed. For a moment he was lost for words, and then he started again, as the full force of what Izzy had said hit home. "This Nick knows about all this does he?" he asked. "Did he put you up to it?"

"Of course not," Izzy said, quickly. "He doesn't know a thing about it."

"Well I'm not having it, you're not riding," Mr. Paterson shouted.

"But Dad," Izzy started, the color draining from her face. "I've got to. Nick's depending on it."

"Well Nick had better *un*depend on it. He's going to think I'm a real idiot after our conversation today, isn't he?" He paused for a moment. "On second thought, you'd better ride tomorrow." Izzy looked astonished, waiting for Mr. Paterson to continue with the conditions that were bound to follow. "But then that horse is going."

"But–" Izzy started. It was worse than she'd imagined possible.

"No buts," Mr. Paterson said, sternly. "I can't believe you've lied to me like this. I'm very disappointed in you, Izzy, and your mother will be too."

"But Dad, you can't tell Mom," Izzy wailed, the tears welling in her eyes. "Ple-ee-ase. Please wait until things are over. She'll be so disappointed."

Mr. Paterson looked thoughtful and made a snap decision. "You're right, your mother's got enough on her plate at the moment. No, perhaps I won't tell her yet," he started. "I'll wait till it's all over. But she'll have to know afterward."

Izzy hung her head, shamefully.

"You've let us down badly," Mr. Paterson said, shaking his head. "And you can phone this Nick and tell him we'll be driving you to the trials too. You're not going with the rest of the team. Now that I've heard what you're capable of, I wouldn't put anything past you," Mr. Paterson continued, not allowing Izzy to interrupt.

It was all too much – the confession, the confusion, the scolding. Before Izzy knew it, the tears were streaming down her cheeks.

"I have to phone Kate," she said, anything to escape from the room. "At least she won't be annoyed with me." And quickly she ran down the hallway.

Anxiously, Izzy twisted the telephone cord in her fingers as she dialed Kate's number. And then Izzy's heart sank as she heard the dull, busy signal at the other end.

She put the phone down in despair. She'd have to

try her again tomorrow. Right now all she wanted to do was curl up in bed. She hurried upstairs and closed her bedroom door behind her. Izzy wiped her eyes with her sleeve. It didn't really matter if she won or lost at Hawthorn tomorrow now – not if she couldn't keep Midnight anyway. And yet somehow it did. Somehow it mattered very much how she rode tomorrow. She had to show her parents what had made her do it. She had to prove that Midnight had been worth it.

****

"Come on, Kate. If you don't get out of that bathtub you'll disappear down the drain."

"Coming Mom," Kate answered. She shivered and reached for her bath towel before stepping out of the tub. She wondered if Izzy had gotten around to telling her parents yet. It was the first time they'd argued since the night Midnight had gotten colic and Kate felt badly.

Kate sighed as she squeezed the toothpaste onto her brush. If she was totally honest with herself, it wasn't all Izzy's fault either. There was something else that had caused the argument – something she hadn't been able to tell Izzy. Winning at Hawthorn had been all that Kate had thought about for the last few months and secretly she'd been thrilled to be picked to ride... more thrilled than anyone might have imagined. Deep down she wanted to win more than anything in the world. And yet now she knew she couldn't. She had to let Izzy win. She had to let Izzy have that chance to keep her horse. She knew how much it meant to her, and there'd be plenty of other horse trials for her.

Biting her lip, Kate pulled on her pajamas and walked across the landing to her bedroom.

"I thought you'd fallen asleep in there," Alex called cheerfully.

"No, I-I." For a brief moment, Kate was close to confiding in her brother and telling him everything – how Izzy didn't have the money to pay for Midnight's keep, how she was counting on winning at Hawthorn, but then Kate stopped herself.

"Nervous are you?" Alex asked.

"Something like that," Kate sighed.

"Don't worry. You'll be all right. Just try and get a good night's sleep."

"Thanks Alex," Kate said, wearily.

Closing the door behind her, she exhaled slowly. Izzy was probably telling her parents about Midnight at that very moment. Kate hoped they were being as understanding as she'd said they would be. What if they weren't? Kate was guiltily aware that it was only at her suggestion that Izzy was telling them.

Kate's head was spinning now, and there was a gnawing, sickly feeling in the pit of her stomach. What would Nick say when she messed things up at the trials tomorrow? Hadn't he said before that if Feather won it would make her quite a valuable horse? Still, Kate's mind was made up. She and Feather couldn't win. She just wouldn't let them.

12

HAWTHORN

When Kate's alarm went off the next morning, a tingle of excitement ran through her body. Hawthorn! And then her heart sank as she saw her new navy show jacket hanging ominously on the closet door and remembered what lay ahead of her.

Kate looked out of the window. It was a clear, crisp day. Cold, but perfect weather for riding all the same. Under normal circumstances, she would have been delighted to be going to a horse trials, but today was different. Unwillingly, she dragged herself out of bed and down the stairs into the kitchen where her mother was pouring a cup of tea.

"Are you all right, Kate?" she asked. "Feeling nervous?"

"Hmm, not too bad," Kate answered, shrugging her

shoulders. She wished everyone would stop asking her that. It only made it ten times worse.

"What time are you leaving for the stables?" her mother went on.

"Oh in ten minutes or so. Whenever Alex is up," Kate replied. She was in no hurry to get there, but she didn't want to tell her mother that. She looked up as Alex came bounding down the stairs.

"You look nice, Kate," he said. "All set and raring to go?"

"Sort of," she said, gruffly.

"Ooh, grumpy too! Who got out of bed on the wrong side?" He turned to his mother. "Probably just last minute nerves," he said, cupping his hand over his mouth, but saying it loudly enough so that Kate could hear.

Ignoring him, Kate got up from the kitchen bench, and wandered aimlessly into the hallway. She stopped to check her appearance in the mirror. That would have to do. Fleetingly, she wondered why Izzy hadn't called her last night.

"Come on, Kate," Alex called. "I'm ready, and you'll be late otherwise."

Kate looked at her watch. Seven o'clock. Grabbing her riding hat, she followed Alex out of the house and unpadlocked her bike.

"See you later," Alex called to his mother. "Quick." He turned to Kate as the ring of the telephone sounded from the house. "It's probably Nick checking to see if we've left."

And so the two of them rode away. When Mrs.

Paterson came running out of the house to say that Izzy was on the phone, it was too late to catch them.

"Kate, Kate," she called. But Alex and Kate were already pedaling away at top speed. Mrs. Hardy shrugged her shoulders and hurried back into the house.

****

"I don't believe it." Izzy slammed the phone down, crossly. She'd just missed Kate. If only she'd gotten up a few minutes earlier she would have caught her.

"Nervous Izzy?" her mother asked, looking up from her cup of tea.

"A little," she answered. She felt funny pretending to her mother that everything was all right when it wasn't. "Could we go soon?" Izzy asked, quick to change the conversation.

"Why? What's the hurry? Your dressage test isn't till eleven is it?" her mother answered.

"No, but I want to watch Kate in hers," Izzy answered. "She's on at nine, so the sooner I can get there the better."

"All right, all right. I'll just give your dad a shout and then we'll get going. Max, Max," Mrs. Paterson called for her husband.

"One minute." A reply came from the depths of his study, and then he appeared.

"Come on, Max. This is Izzy's day," Mrs. Paterson said, smiling. Izzy reddened as her father looked across and gave her a stern look.

Waiting by the door, Izzy twisted uncomfortably in her riding jacket. It was Kate's old one and a little on the tight side. She would rather be in her scruffy old parka any day.

At last they were ready, and Izzy got into the car. Mr. Paterson pulled out of the driveway.

"Do you know where we're going, Izzy?" Mrs. Paterson asked.

"Yes," Izzy answered, grabbing the road atlas from beside her. "We need to take the road to Ash Hill, skirt around Littleford and then it's straight all the way to Hawthorn." She tucked a piece of hair behind her ear as she spoke.

"Easy then," her mother said. "We should be there in plenty of time. So why don't you tell us how these trials work then, Izzy."

An uncomfortable silence pervaded the car as Izzy took a deep breath and tried to make a start. "Well," she began. "The main event of the day is the Open Cup. There'll be lots of older riders competing for that. It's the last qualifying event for the Trentdown Trials. I'm in the Junior Cup for under 12s. It's a new sort of event – the first of its kind to be held at Hawthorn. You ride in dressage, show jumping and cross-country and the scores in each of them are then added up."

All of this talk had managed to distract Izzy and she hadn't noticed the traffic bunching up ahead of them. She looked at her watch. It was already quarter to nine.

"Uh oh," her mother sighed.

"What is it?" Izzy asked.

"Traffic," Mr. Paterson groaned.

"I knew we should have left earlier," Izzy cried as they drew up behind a large trailer and came to a grinding halt. "I'm going to miss Kate's dressage now."

"Be patient, Izzy," her mother said, calmly. "I'm sure it'll get going in a minute."

But Mrs. Paterson's words weren't reassuring to Izzy.

"It's not far now. Look, there you are," Mrs. Paterson pointed. "Horse Trials one mile."

"But the traffic's not moving. I'm going to have to get out and walk," Izzy wailed.

"You'll do no such thing." Mr. Paterson looked stern. "Just calm down."

But Izzy was finding it hard to sit still. She should have known something like this would happen. Vacantly, she stared out of the window. The traffic was starting to move again and Izzy could vaguely hear the muffled sound of a loud speaker in the distance. She looked across the grass at the show jumping ring, surrounded by green and white striped stands. They hadn't even reached the entrance yet. Izzy screwed her hands up into little balls, clenching them and unclenching them.

"Sorry," she gasped. "It's five to nine. I've just got

to get out. I'll meet you by the secretary's tent at eleven-thirty."

And before they could stop her, Izzy had leapt out of the car, and was running blindly down the road. Sprinting along the grass verge, she pushed past people hurrying to the trials on foot.

"Excuse me, excuse me," she cried, stumbling forward as she raced. She really should stop and ask someone where she'd find the dressage ring, but there just wasn't time for that. And then it all happened so quickly. One minute she was hurtling forward, the next she had put her foot in a hole, and was crashing to the ground.

"Ow." She grimaced, rubbing her ankle.

"Are you OK?" A woman called over.

"I'm fine," Izzy said, angry at herself for falling.

Bravely, she got to her feet and cringed. She felt a sharp, searing pain in her foot. Tears sprang up in her eyes as she struggled to stand.

"I'll be all right in a moment," she said to the woman, wincing as she tried to put some weight on the injured foot.

"I don't think you will be. It looks as though you might have twisted your ankle."

Wheezing to catch her breath, Izzy looked at her watch. It was two minutes after nine. Too late. She'd have missed Kate's test, and now the tears she'd desperately been trying to hold back all morning, began to run down her face.

"I'm late to see my friend ride," she explained. "And I'm going to lose my horse too. I wanted my parents to see how good he was," she babbled. "My ankle's throbbing, and I'm supposed to be in the dressage ring at eleven."

"Don't worry," the lady said kindly. "I think we'd better get you to the first aid tent as quickly as possible. Put your arm over my shoulder and lean on me. There, that's it. Somehow I don't think you'll be riding today."

****

As Kate came out of the ring, she hoped against hope that Nick hadn't seen her performance. She had certainly ridden badly enough to take them out of the running. Her first circle had been more of a square and then she had circled at C instead of E – that was two penalty points straight off for a change of course. Feather had swished her tail and seemed confused, but still she had obeyed Kate's instructions.

At least that was all over with now. Looking up, Kate saw Alex heading straight for her.

"You were terrible. What happened?" he demanded, in his typical blunt style.

"I guess I just got nervous," Kate said quickly, turning away so that he couldn't see her face.

"You're in eighth place. You've completely blown it, Kate. I thought you'd be up there with the leaders after the dressage."

"I know, I know, don't keep going on about it, Alex," Kate said hastily, jumping to the ground and burying her head in Feather's neck.

"Where's Nick?" she asked anxiously.

"Not sure." Alex looked blank. "He said he'd be watching, but he's not going to be too pleased with that performance."

"Any sign of Izzy?" Kate asked, ignoring his comment.

"No, not a squeak," Alex said. "We've all been wondering where she is. Nick said she'd be here by nine."

"Probably hasn't told her parents yet," Kate muttered under her breath.

"What was that?" Alex asked.

"Oh nothing," Kate answered, tiredly. She felt irritable. She had given up everything so Izzy would have a good chance of winning – Nick's opinion of her, Feather's chances, her own chances. And Izzy didn't even have the decency to turn up on time.

Kate was kicking a stone around the ground when there was an announcement over the speaker that brought her back to earth with a jolt.

"Could the parents of Izzy Paterson come to the first aid tent immediately?"

Kate's heart skipped a beat. What was going on? Without a second thought, she set off, darting this way and that, dodging in and out of the crowds as she ran. Stopping for a moment to catch her breath, Kate caught sight of the first aid tent and plunged inside.

Izzy wasn't alone. Nick was already there and a nurse hovered in the background. Kate just caught the tail end of what Nick was saying.

"So that's it. I'm afraid you're not going to be able to ride Midnight, Izzy..."

****

Kate blinked. What was going on? What was wrong with Izzy?

"Kate, just the person we needed to see." Nick looked grim. "I'm sorry I missed you and Feather, but I heard the result. You didn't do too well, did you?"

"Not really," Kate said, sheepishly. "Six penalty points."

"And I'm afraid Izzy's twisted her ankle," Nick explained. "She won't be able to ride Midnight today."

"Izzy! How on earth did that happen?" Kate cried.

"I was late getting here," Izzy said. Her face was stained with tears. "We were stuck in traffic, so I got out of the car and was running along the road and... well, I fell. Anyway, never mind that," Izzy said. "Nick's got something to talk to you about."

Kate looked puzzled and turned to look at Nick, waiting for an explanation.

"I won't beat around the bush," Nick said, quickly.

"You've clearly blown your chances with Feather, so I've suggested to Izzy that you take over for her and ride Midnight. Izzy's agreed, but it's up to you now. There isn't much time, so what do you think?"

"Well, I don't know," Kate said, looking from one face to the other.

"Don't mind me," Izzy said, kindly. "I'd rather you rode him than not. I can't very well, and besides, it'll give you a second crack at the trophy.

A second crack at the trophy. Kate was torn between being devastated for Izzy and thrilled for herself. Quickly, she pulled herself together.

"OK, I'll do it," she said, determinedly.

"Good, well, I'll leave you both to discuss things then," Nick said. "I've got to go and get permission for the change of rider at the secretary's tent." He turned to Kate. "There isn't much time before Midnight's dressage test. Meet me back at the van in exactly half an hour."

Kate nodded and turned back to Izzy. "Do you mind Izzy?" she asked.

"No, it's fine, Kate," said Izzy. "You see, being able to ride at the trials wouldn't make any difference to me anyway."

"What? But what do you mean?" Kate was flabbergasted. "Everything's riding on it."

"Not really," Izzy answered her. "Not any more. You see I told Dad everything, and he's going to make me sell Midnight anyway. It wouldn't make much difference whether I win or lose, so don't think about me. You just go out there and do your best for your own sake."

"Sure I'll do that Izzy, but–"

Izzy held up her hand to silence her friend. "There's nothing more to be done," she said, tiredly. "I can't bear to talk about it any more. Now I'm going to have to wait for my parents to explain what's happened."

Kate patted her friend on the shoulder and left the tent.

13

SHOW JUMPING

The show jumping ring stood quiet and empty as the last of the competitors finished their tests over at the dressage ring. Gaily-painted flags swung in the breeze. Kate hadn't ridden Midnight too badly in the dressage – they were in third place, but there was still a long way to go. Kate wondered how Izzy was. She hadn't turned up to watch her, so maybe she was having a tougher time with her parents than she'd counted on.

Ducking under the fence, Kate looked at the course. The jumps weren't enormous by show jumping standards, but she would need to jump them clear if she wanted to catch the leader. She was quiet as she walked the course, contemplating it all. She looked at her watch – nearly time now. She should go and tack up Midnight. Quickly, she headed back to the horse van. The showground was busy, as she went on her way – each of the riders getting ready for their different events.

"You ought to go and warm up," Nick called over to where she stood. "You're on in the show jumping ring in twenty minutes."

"I know," Kate answered, hurrying over to tack up Midnight.

Quickly, she tightened the girth and jumped into the saddle. As she walked over to the practice ring, she ran over the course in her mind. She felt strangely distant as she watched the riders popping back and forth over the practice jump. Poor, poor Izzy. Kate took a deep breath. She had to do well. She simply had to show everyone what Midnight could do.

Kate squinted into the distance. They were up to number twenty-two – just two more riders ahead of her. Time was going so painfully slowly, she couldn't bear it. All she wanted was to get it over and done with. Quietly, she trotted over to the ring, waiting for her turn. Then she heard Midnight's number being announced and rode into the ring. As the sound of the bell echoed around the grounds, she pushed Midnight on toward the first jump.

"Come on boy," she cried, urging him onto the brush. The black horse responded willingly and they cleared the jump with ease. Kate rode him hard at the shark's teeth. Touchdown and clear, and now it was the combination.

Carefully, she eased him over the fence. Clear! Now onto the parallel bars. They glided over the jump in quick, easy strides and headed for the triple.

Jump... clear, jump... clear.... jump... clear...

The crowd was quiet as the pair soared over the jumps in swift succession. Midnight didn't even hesitate as Kate rode him around the course. He snorted excitedly as he approached the gate and landed lightly. There were only two jumps left that lay between them and a clear round.

Kate turned Midnight for the stile, and he soared over the jump with inches to spare. Now there was only the wall. Kate didn't hesitate as she swung Midnight wide, giving him enough berth to look at the jump. Midnight sailed through the air as if it was invisible and they cantered through the finish to a round of applause.

Almost immediately Kate was surrounded by a circle of excited faces.

"Clear round, Kate," the Sandy Lane team cried.

"Yes, well done, Kate," said Nick. Kate smiled weakly. Anxiously, she looked around her as she jumped to the ground.

"Have you seen Izzy?" she asked Alex.

"She's with her parents," he answered, raising his eyebrows. "It seems she has kind of a lot to discuss with them."

"Do you know what exactly?" Kate asked, nervously.

"Well no," said Alex. "She muttered something about Midnight's board."

"That's all you know?" Kate asked.

"Well, what more is there to know?" Alex said. "You and Izzy have both been so secretive lately. Are you up to something?" he asked, suspiciously.

"Of course we're not," Kate said, narrowly avoiding Alex's eye, as she led Midnight off by the reins.

14

CROSS-COUNTRY

It didn't taken Kate long to find Izzy, nor for Izzy to relate her woeful tale. She'd had a lot of explaining to do when her parents had arrived at the first aid tent – not least of all to her mother when her father spilled the beans about her deception. Mrs. Paterson hadn't taken it that well. She'd been as adamant as Izzy's father that Midnight had to be sold. Izzy couldn't bear the atmosphere in the tent and had sneaked away as soon as possible.

Now, as Kate and Izzy leaned on the fence by the cross-country course, they both felt gloomy. Wearily, Izzy clapped her hands together as competitor number forty-three rode through the finish to a round of applause.

"Come on. Don't worry, Kate," Izzy said. "You should be the one trying to cheer me up not the other way around."

"I know, I know," said Kate. "I suppose I just thought that your parents would help you, that they'd come up with something."

"And they have," Izzy said. "They've agreed to pay Nick what I owe him – nearly a month's board – it's pretty generous," she said, suddenly feeling annoyed. It was all right for her to criticize her parents, but she didn't like the thought of someone else doing it.

"But how can you say that? They're still making you sell Midnight," Kate cried.

Izzy shrugged her shoulders. "I don't know why you thought it would be any different," she said, trying to keep the choking feeling out of her voice. "And at least you get to ride him at the trials," she said, gruffly.

"Look Izzy, you said you wanted me to," Kate said, hurt by her friend's tone of voice. Suddenly she felt an overwhelming urge to tell Izzy how she had sacrificed her own chances with Feather. But she stopped herself. It would only be rubbing salt into the wound. Besides, it couldn't change things now. And then there was an announcement over the loud speaker that caused Kate to start.

"And that was the leader, Justin Rolph on Light Fandango in four minutes and thirty seconds," the speaker announced.

Both friends looked up. Kate went quiet.

"Great," she said despondently. "I'll never beat that."

"Of course you will, Kate," Izzy said confidently.

"But it was so fast," said Kate.

"But you only have to ride four minutes fifteen to make up the two points," Izzy said.

Kate looked doubtful. Izzy shrugged her shoulders and turned away. It was a few minutes before she said anything.

"Hmm, well perhaps you're right, Kate. In fact, you ought to have practiced a little harder at Sandy Lane – after all, cross-country's never been your strong point, has it?" she said, looking down so that Kate couldn't see her biting her bottom lip. "I always used to beat you hands down," Izzy continued.

"What do you mean you used to beat me hands down?" Kate was indignant now. "Only because you used to almost break Midnight's neck in the process," she shouted. "Well, we'll soon see about that."

And marching off, she stomped across the showground, leaving Izzy standing alone. It was just the reaction Izzy had wanted.

"Yes, we will soon see about that, Kate," she said, limping off slowly with her crutches.

****

Kate gritted her teeth as she and Midnight stood in the starting box, patiently waiting for the official to signal the start of the cross-country. The wind was blowing up around them. She'd have to go very fast if they were to have any chance of winning. Kate held her breath. The starter counted her down and they were off.

The whoops of the crowd echoed in her ears as they thundered to the first jump and galloped into the trees. Skirting through the woody copse, turning this way and that, Kate navigated a clear route through to the other side and then they were at the sloping rails.

"Come on, Midnight," she cried determinedly as she collected him for the log into the water. "Steady now, easy does it."

The black horse jumped into the water and splashed through the brook. Leaning forward in the saddle, Kate urged him up the other side. His hooves sank deep into the mud as he struggled to keep his footing, but he was out clear and now they galloped the turn for the fallen tree.

Over that, and nimbly Kate turned for the drop into the creek, leaning back to take the weight off Midnight's front legs, down into the dip and up the other side for the rails. The mud sprayed up in Kate's face and she spluttered, breathlessly.

It was a long and hard gallop to the next fence but so far so good, they hadn't made a wrong step. Bracing herself for the tires, Kate pushed her seat down deep into the saddle.

"Come on," she cried, riding hard in the approach. The gutsy black horse didn't baulk at the solid jump. With a huge leap, he hauled himself over it with inches to spare. Kate didn't even give him time to think about what he had just cleared as she turned him for the low gate and surged on over the trough. Halfway home. Kate was starting to feel confident now.

Sailing over the stone wall, they headed for the next fence. Kate drove Midnight on with her heels and he rose to the challenge, tucking his legs neatly up under him. Now it was Devil's Ditch. Kate could sense that he was tiring. Down the bank, over the log pile and onto the triple bar. Kate rode at the middle of the jump, steadying Midnight for the takeoff and they landed lightly.

Just two more jumps. The double oxer was now in their sights. Up and over and touchdown. They were clear. Just one more jump. The black horse swished his tail as they flew across the turf and sprinted through the finish.

Crossing the line, Kate drew to a halt and collapsed in a heap on Midnight's neck. Had she done it? Gasping to catch her breath, she didn't even look up at the sound of voices around her.

Before she knew it, she was surrounded by Nick and the Sandy Lane gang. It was some time before she'd even got her breath back to speak.

"Are you OK?" Nick asked, patting her on the back. "Say something."

For once Kate was lost for words. "How did I do?" she croaked.

"Terrific. You rode incredibly well," Alex said, as Kate slithered to the ground, her legs quivering like jelly beneath her.

"But was it enough?" she gasped.

"We'll have to wait and see," said Alex.

"Kate Hardy and Midnight. Four minutes and twelve seconds," the loud speaker announced.

"You've done it! You've done it!" the Sandy Lane team cried. But there was only one face Kate wanted to see.

"There," Kate said, proudly, as Izzy and her parents strode over. "Who said I couldn't do it?" she said.

"I didn't doubt it for a moment," Izzy grinned, patting Midnight's neck.

And suddenly everything dawned on Kate. "You!" she said, pointing her finger at Izzy. "You only said it to spur me on."

"And it worked didn't it?" Izzy said. "Kate, meet Mom and Dad."

"Hello," Kate said, remembering her manners in front of Izzy's parents. She looked at their smiling faces and was suddenly puzzled. Izzy had just been told she had to sell her horse and she looked positively glowing. Her parents didn't look that annoyed either. And now, here were Nick and her own parents arriving to add to the crowd.

"Great job, Kate," Nick started. "You rode fantastically. And as for Midnight – well, not bad for an old fellow," he said, patting his neck.

Kate's parents stepped forward.

"Yes well done, Kate." Mrs. Hardy beamed. Kate looked pleased, but then she remembered that there was something more pressing that she needed to know about. What was happening to Midnight? Kate looked at Izzy waiting for an explanation.

"What's going on, Izzy?" she started.

"I can keep Midnight," Izzy said, calmly.

Before Izzy even had a chance to explain further, the loud speaker made another announcement.

"Kate Hardy and Midnight are the overall winners of the Junior Hawthorn Cup," came the result.

"I've won? I've truly won at Hawthorn?" Kate said, momentarily distracted. "I don't believe it."

"Well, you'd better believe it," said Izzy, pushing Kate into the ring. "Stuffy old Major Benrick is waiting to present your prize to you. Hurry up." Izzy smiled. "Go on, they're calling your name."

"But what's going on?"

"Don't worry Kate. I'll explain it all when you get back. Just go out there and get that cup. If you don't hurry they'll give it to someone else," Izzy teased. "All you need to know is that Midnight's here to stay," she smiled. "But it's kind of a long story..."

Kate remounted and rode off slowly, burning with curiosity. "I'll deal with you later," she called back to Izzy as she rode into the ring. But she wasn't really annoyed, not when she had just won. She was first at Hawthorn! As Kate accepted her cup and galloped the victory lap, she could only smile.

15

MIDNIGHT TO STAY

"For she's a jolly good fellow, for she's a jolly good fellow, for she's a jolly good fe-e-llow..."

Nick covered his ears to drown out the singing as he drove the Sandy Lane team back to the yard. But he didn't try to stop them. He was pleased they were happy – first place at Hawthorn was excellent. Izzy and Kate were tucked away in the back, out of earshot of the lively group in the front.

"I'm sorry you didn't get to ride at the trials, Izzy," Kate started.

"That's the least of my worries," Izzy answered. "Who cares about all that when I can keep Midnight? There'll be plenty of other trials for us."

"So tell me again exactly how it happened – and slowly this time," Kate said.

"Are you sure you want the whole story?" Izzy asked tiredly. It had been a long day for her.

"Of course I do," Kate said smiling. "From start to finish."

"Hmm." Izzy took a deep breath. "Well, this is all third hand remember. I only know what happened from Mom, but I'll tell you anyway. After I sneaked out of the first aid tent, it seems Dad went off to find Nick. He told him all about the deception, expecting Nick to be as furious as he was, and instead Nick stuck up for me... said that I was a gutsy kid and had enough talent to fill a stables." Izzy blushed at the words of praise.

"Anyway, Dad couldn't believe it," Izzy went on, her enthusiasm spilling out into her speech. "He was really miffed that Nick was sticking up for me and then when Nick said he would be prepared to buy Midnight if Dad couldn't afford to keep him, it was the final straw. Dad jumped in and agreed to let me keep him immediately."

"That's awesome," said Kate.

"Yes," Izzy smiled happily. "But there are conditions attached – it wasn't a complete breeze. Midnight and I are on a six month trial period, so I've got to work really hard at school to improve my grades, although, Mom says I've as good as got him," Izzy babbled, happily. "And there was something else that swayed things too."

Kate waited patiently as Izzy went on.

"I think that the details of it all sort of intrigued him," she started. "Me wanting Midnight so badly...

keeping him secret... the colic... He said it all had the makings of a great book!"

Kate laughed as Izzy's story unfolded and the van turned sharply into the stable grounds.

The dark was closing in as the horses were unloaded and it wasn't long before Midnight was back in his stall. The two girls stood leaning on the door, watching the black horse eat from his haynet.

"It's really strange how things turn out, isn't it?" Izzy said thoughtfully.

"What do you mean?" Kate puzzled.

"Well, if I hadn't seen that ad at the post office, I'd never have met Mrs. Charlwood, or Midnight for that matter. I'd never have found Sandy Lane, or met all of you... it was really a whole series of chance happenings – one leading to the other. And who'd have thought that I'd be able to keep Midnight after all. I know I was lucky. I shouldn't really have been able to get away with it," Izzy began.

"Now, you're not going to get serious on me, are you?" Kate groaned.

"No," Izzy laughed. "Nothing like that. It's just that... well, never mind." Izzy stopped herself.

"No, go on, Izzy. Say what you were going to say," Kate said, intrigued.

"Well, it's just funny how you can be so wrong about people too," Izzy started. "Do you remember when I first arrived at Sandy Lane for instance?"

"How could I forget it?" Kate answered.

"Well, you've have to remember I was upset that I had been separated from Midnight for so long," Izzy

111

went on. "And I'd had the flu and then you were so awful... so cold."

"Me, *cold*?"

The two girls turned and frowned at each other. It was just at that moment that Midnight lifted his head and whinnied loudly, bringing their squabble to a close.

Kate looked at Izzy. Izzy looked at Kate, and they both burst out laughing.

A Horse for the Summer by Michelle Bates

The first title in the Sandy Lane Stables series

There was a frantic whinny and the sound of drumming hooves reverberated around the yard as Chancey pranced down the ramp. He was certainly on his toes, but he didn't look like the sleek, well turned-out horse that Tom remembered seeing last season. He was still unclipped and his shabby winter coat was flecked with foam as feverishly he pawed the ground. No one knew what to say...

When Tom is lent a prize-winning show jumper for the summer, things don't turn out quite as he hoped. Chancey is wild and unpredictable and Tom is forced to start training him in secret. But the days of summer are numbered and Chancey isn't Tom's to keep forever. At some point, he will have to give him back...

The Runaway Pony by Susannah Leigh

The second title in the Sandy Lane Stables series

Angry shouting and the crunch of hooves on gravel made Jess spin around sharply. Careening toward her, wild-eyed with fear and long tail flying behind, was a palomino pony. It was completely out of control. Jess's heart began to pound and her breath came in sharp gasps, but almost without thinking she held out her arms...

When the bridleless and riderless palomino pony clatters into the yard, no one is more surprised than Jess. Hot on the pony's hooves comes a man waving a halter. Jess helps him catch the pony and sends them on their way. Little is she to know what far-reaching consequences her simple actions will have...

Strangers at the Stables by Michelle Bates

The third title in the Sandy Lane Stables series

...Thoughts jostled around in Rosie's mind as she crossed the yard. She couldn't believe how many things had gone wrong in the couple of weeks Nick and Sarah had been gone. She needed time to think. There was something worrying her, right at the back of her mind... something that held the key to it all. But what was it?

When the owners of Sandy Lane are called away, everyone still expects the stable to run smoothly in their absence. No one is prepared for all the things that happen over the next few weeks. There isn't time to get help, the children of Sandy Lane have to act fast, if they want to save their stables...